Dedication

This goes to Dan, Ruth, the Kapanke family, and the entire Loggers organization. Without your amazing support, this dream would not have become real.

Thank you with all my heart.

I CROSSE MY HEART

CityScapes: Wisconsin

CJ Bower

Chapter 1

I never should have moved into that apartment.

Kallie exhaled a sigh as she gazed out over the panorama. She was glad that their time with their Roommates from Hell was almost over. When she and her best friend Amy had moved into the apartment with Ingrid and Zoe last year, they'd had no clue the nightmare that had awaited them.

"Would moving back in with Mom and Dad be considered defeat?" she asked the crickets chirping on the other side of the chain-link fence. "Or just a retreat and regroup?"

The underbrush rustled in front of her, and a fat cottontail appeared briefly as it ducked between the bushes.

The view from the Grandad Bluff Overlook never failed to take Kallie's breath as she took in the sights of the city in the late-May dusk. She stood at the rail and gazed at her favorite natural spectacle, letting the peaceful scenery quiet her inner turmoil. The location a popular destination for locals and tourists alike, she'd been one of several visitors the last time she'd ventured to the top of the overlook.

Tonight, however, she reveled in the solitude. The chaos from her roommates cut in on what little time she'd had to study. She'd nearly tanked her last final, which jeopardized her goal of graduating with honors and her chances of getting hired by a top clinical research laboratory.

Glancing up at the sky, she imagined her uncle smiling down at her. "I'm sorry, Uncle Seth. I'm trying, but my classes have just gotten too hard. I don't know if I can do it."

Seth had been the one to inspire her to choose Clinical Laboratory Science as a major. He'd passed away two years ago from non-Hodgkin's Lymphoma, which made her decide to learn as much about the disease as she possibly could. Like many before her, she wanted to find a cure for that, and many other cancers.

She rolled her shoulders to ease the tension in her back.

From her vantage point Kallie could see two of the three states in the Mississippi River Valley, with Minnesota directly across from her. Down the river, the headlands of Iowa were indiscernible in the rapidly disappearing light.

The late spring air was balmy as she studied the landscape, birds chirping in the serene atmosphere as they began settling for the night. La Crosse glowed below as lights winked on along the streets. Directly across the city, the Cass and Cameron Bridges spanned the main channel of the Mississippi as boats and barges glided along the tranquil waterway. To her far right, open waters of the Black River glistened as Mother Nature serenaded her. Sighing, she closed her eyes as her thoughts inevitably returned to her current sticky situation.

Moving in with Zoe and Ingrid had been a huge mistake. With no regard to either Kallie or Amy, Zoe had had male visitors stop by at all hours, day or night, and none of them had stayed more than a couple hours each.

More than once, Kallie had caught Zoe wearing her clothes, and she was pretty sure one of them had stolen cash from her wallet. She'd snuck back into Zoe's room to retrieve her clothes. However, without proof, she kept quiet about the cash.

The peaceful vista soothed away some of Kallie's post-finals stress, and reminded her of how small she was in the grand scheme of life. When she opened her eyes, dusk had fallen. The craggy cliffs fanned the last of the sun's waning rays. Reds and oranges spread like fingers, fading into the blues and indigos of twilight. White and red lights roamed the grid of streets as her fellow city slickers rushed toward their destinations in the bumper-to-bumper traffic through the marshland; a quiet oasis in a bustling town. She could just make out the towering spire of the St. Joseph the Workman Cathedral in the heart of downtown.

Crickets ceased their songs as rustling from the rocks on the other side of the fence below startled her. Kallie jumped back, her heart pounding. The metal hand rails played a light song from the gusts of breeze passing between them, at the same time sending her long hair in all directions. The waning twilight made it difficult to see more than a few feet in any direction, and she couldn't tell where the noise came from. The floodlights shining up the flag pole in front of the park shelter gave minimal assistance. *Time to tell the Wicked Witches they're on their own.*

Both she and Amy had made the decision to move at the end of May, and had spent the last two days relocating their stuff. Zoe and Ingrid spent all day yesterday at the spa, and had made a road trip to the Mall Of America in Bloomington, Minnesota for a day of shopping.

Though they were all mostly broke college students, Zoe seemed to have money to burn. An insane amount of extra cash, to be honest.

Kallie suspected Zoe was employing dishonest means of obtaining it.

Since all of the bills were in Ingrid's name, Kallie felt no guilt in leaving them in the lurch. As far as she was concerned, it was no less than what they deserved. She had a bad feeling about why Zoe had convinced Ingrid to put all of the utilities in her name. Kallie only hoped Ingrid would figure it out sooner rather than later, and ditch Zoe. The woman was bad news, and Kallie was glad to finally be rid of her.

With one last look over the incredible view, Kallie headed for her ageing truck. Eyes on the sidewalk, she followed the path around the building. Without warning, she collided with the solid wall of a man's chest. Two strong hands caught her before she hit the ground.

"I – I'm sorry," she said, giving the man a cursory glance as she tried to sidestep him. "I wasn't watching where I was going."

The man held her captive, both literally and figuratively, his smile dazzling in the artificial lights. "No, I'm the one who's sorry. I wasn't watchin', either."

His companions snickered. Kallie ignored them, her attention on the guy she'd bumped into. His aftershave held a citrusy note and his voice carried a gently rolling Texan drawl.

"Are you all right?" He steadied her, then dropped his hands into his pockets.

Kallie nodded, a shiver snaking down her spine. She wasn't sure if it was from fear or the thrill of being held by him. He was gorgeous, with wavy dark hair that glistened beneath the halo of lights beaming from the shelter, and he hadn't stumbled when she'd crashed into him.

Common sense finally kicked in. Taking a step back she shoved her hand into her pocket and palmed her keys, sliding one key between each of her clenched fingers with the sharp ends pointing out. "Yes, thank you. I'm fine."

"I'm glad." Amusement sparkled in his dark gaze, and one corner of his lips kicked up into a sexy half-smile.

A wave of uneasiness sent goosebumps across her flesh as she recognized the inherent danger for a woman alone on the top of a cliff surrounded by four guys. Though they made no advance toward her, she gave them a wide berth. Holding her breath, she moved to sidestep him again, and sighed when he made no move to stop her.

"Enjoy the rest of your night." Kallie hurried to where her truck sat, ignoring the catcalls trailing in her wake.

She climbed in and locked the door, then fastened her seatbelt and started the motor. Shoving the transmission into gear, she barked the tires as she peeled out of the parking lot. Only to end up slamming the brakes when she came up to a blind corner where the road disappeared up the incline.

Kallie kept her pace slow as she followed the rest of the quiet lane dividing a dense forest until she came to the end of the road. The lights and smells from the Alpine Inn Bar and

Grill greeted her as she braked to a stop at the T-intersection. Making sure the coast was clear, she turned onto Bliss Road and kept her truck beneath the speed limit as she coasted down the narrow, winding lane. Familiar with the street layout, her mind drifted back to the hot guy she'd run into, and her body still tingled from her collision against him.

I wonder if I'll see him again.

****

Rafe's palms still tingled with the feel of the woman's flesh long after she'd fled. Lucas, David and Justin gave him a hard time, but he expected it. Hell, he welcomed it. He'd have done the same if one of them had bumped into her.

He leaned against the fence with his back to the city as he listened to his teammates gossip about the pretty lady. They were all in La Crosse for summer baseball with the Loggers. Rafe hoped to improve his skills so he could help his team win a national title next season. However, his ultimate goal was to play for a professional baseball team.

Needing a few moments alone to gather his thoughts, Rafe strolled down the sidewalk to the lower observation deck. The view offered an unfettered panorama as the city lay beneath him. Dusk gave way to night, with only a rosy glow remaining on the horizon where the sun had finally set and stars winking on overhead. He thought of his mission and why he'd signed the contract with the Loggers.

The Northwoods League had become one of the frontrunners for producing power players. Rafe closed his eyes, recalling some of the huge names that had come from the Loggers' previous teams. Max Scherzer, Chris Sale, Andrew Knapp, Eric Thames, Matt Chapman. Rafe hoped to add his name to that growing list in two or three short years.

Turning, he looked out over the city, not paying attention to the view as his thoughts returned to her. Her glittering eyes, her dark hair, her beautiful smile. Her intoxicating scent. *Would her hair feel as soft and silky as it looked?* Rafe breathed in deep as the crickets chirped around him. A hint of something familiar – *his mystery girl?* – teased his senses and he turned, opening his eyes. Disappointment crashed through him when he realized he was alone.

"Guys?" he called out. The crickets ceased their orchestra as he dashed back up the sidewalk leading to the shelter. "Lucas? David? If you don't come out, I'm gonna pound ya!"

"RAAAAAAAAAAARR!"

Rafe jumped. His heart nearly pounded out of his chest as his friends leapt out at him from behind the building. Justin was laughing so hard, he dropped to the ground clutching his sides. Rafe had the intense urge to kick him, but he didn't. The team was short-handed, and needed all available players for the game.

All three of them laughed like fools.

"Dude, you should've seen your face," Lucas chortled. "You damn near pissed your pants!"

Rafe rolled his eyes. "I did not." Despite being the same age as his teammates, growing up as the only child of a dirt-poor single mother made him feel older than his twenty-one years.

"Did too," David chimed in.

"Did not."

David got close to Rafe's face, their noses inches apart. "Did too."

Rafe drew his fist back to throw a punch, with no intention of connecting.

"Whoa." Lucas grabbed Rafe's arm. "No bruises. The season hasn't started yet."

"He deserves it," Rafe countered as he backed away from David. "You all do."

"Ease off, Rafe," Lucas insisted. "David's our starting pitcher for tomorrow's game against Rochester. We're gonna need him."

"Fine," Rafe bit out. He turned on his heel and headed back for the car, "accidentally" catching Justin's shin with the toe of his sneaker. "Payback's a bitch, boys." He looked over his shoulder, never breaking his stride. "Let's go. Tomorrow's gonna be a long day."

Justin rolled to a crouch, then stood as he brushed off his clothes. Good-natured grumbling followed in his wake as they all walked to the car. Rafe slid behind the wheel and slotted the key in the ignition.

"You should've gotten that girl's number," David grumbled as they climbed in and buckled their seatbelts. "She was seriously hot."

Rafe agreed with his teammates, though he didn't feel the need to voice his opinion. "I'll get it next time."

"If there is one," Justin taunted.

Ignoring the taunt, Rafe started the car and headed back down the bluff. He hoped there would be one, but he knew asking her out wouldn't be fair to either of them. His ultimate goal to play in the majors required intense focus and dedication. Even if he did make it to the minors, the odds of getting called up were stacked heavily against him. A relationship between him and the young woman would be nothing more than a summer fling.

A distraction he couldn't afford.

Chapter 2

"I still can't believe Zoe went off half-cocked last night." Kallie handed her ticket to the gate attendant. Her friend, Amy, was behind her as they entered the Copeland Park stadium for the Loggers' season opener.

"I can." Amy scoffed. They passed through a sea of green and white as fans gathered in the front entry. "She thinks the whole world revolves around her. Even Ingrid worships the ground she walks on. It's disgusting."

Kallie recalled the venom that Zoe had spewed when she and Ingrid had returned from Minneapolis at nearly midnight, and discovered the apartment practically empty. She'd insisted on waking both Kallie and Amy with a screaming match that had their neighbors emerging from their own apartments. Thankfully no one had called the cops.

Kallie shook her head as she climbed the steps to their seats. "She still didn't need to call me what she did."

"Look on the bright side," Amy said from behind Kallie. "She's Ingrid's problem now. We'll never have to see her again."

"Thank God for small blessings." Kallie found her seat in the top row of the last section. "I'm glad my parents let me move back home."

"Mine did too." Amy sat next to her and threw an arm around her shoulder. "I just wish you and I could move into our own place together."

"Maybe after graduation, when we both start working full-time." Kallie sighed wistfully. "If we're both still in La Crosse."

"Unless it's you and me, forget it," Amy declared. "I'm done putting up with roommates from hell. I'm still convinced Zoe was running a brothel from her bedroom."

Kallie winced. "I think that's why my grades tanked last semester. Between the grooming salon and Zoe's revolving door, I could never get enough quiet time to study."

Shaking off her melancholy, she scanned the stadium, taking in the electric excitement buzzing among the fans. Kallie wasn't a huge baseball fan, but she supported the local teams when she could. And the Loggers always played a great game, no matter which team the scoreboard favored.

The home team congregated near the bullpen in the left-field corner, warming up and doing drills. Rochester's players did the same near the bullpen in front of the right-field corner party deck. A shrill goose honk cried out from somewhere in the stands.

"Oh, great." Kallie turned to Amy. "Someone let the geese out."

Amy chuckled. "Don't they know it's open season?"

"I guess not." Kallie laughed with her friend. "I'm gonna get some food. Want anything?"

Amy shook her head. "I'm good."

Kallie headed down the metal bleachers and toward the stairs. A movement caught her eye. She looked around and saw one of the players waving at her from the field. A nervous giddiness stole over her as she recognized the guy who'd nearly knocked her over last night. He was even more handsome in the light. Instead of turning left at the bottom of the stairs, Kallie followed her instinct and walked around the third-base party deck to the short fence separating the field from the stands.

"Hey, there," the player drawled. "I wasn't sure I'd see you again."

Kallie smiled shyly. "Hi." She was about to say more, but one of his teammates pulled him in a headlock and knuckled the top of his head.

"Rafe missed the opportunity to get your number last night," Headlock Guy said.

"Yeah, what a bonehead." A third guy, just as handsome as Rafe, joined them at the fence. "Can I have it instead?"

"Justin, don't you have a girlfriend back home?"

Justin grinned, elbowing Rafe in the ribs. "What she don't know won't hurt me."

Disgusted by the remark, Kallie turned to leave.

"Wait." Rafe lightly touched her arm. "At least tell me your name."

"Kallie," she stammered softly as electricity crackled from the barely-there contact, which ended almost as soon as it began. Brief though it was, his fingers left a lasting impression on her skin. "I'm Kallie."

"Well, Kallie, it's nice to finally meet you. I'm Rafe." He pointed to his teammates. "Justin and Lucas."

"Nice to meet you guys. Good luck tonight."

Headlock Guy – Lucas – nodded. "Thanks."

"I bet a kiss from you would give him twice the luck," Justin teased.

Rafe's face turned red, and Kallie shook her head. *Boys. They're so predictable.*

"Kiss her already," Lucas said. "Coach is calling us to start the game."

Rafe leaned closer, within kissing distance. "Would you mind if I did?"

Kallie found herself drowning in green eyes dark enough to match the color of his jersey. His eyes had haunted her since last night, and his lips had tempted her to kiss him while she'd been in his arms. Definitely a better memory than the fight that had ensued later that evening. A tremble quaked through her, but not from fear. She'd dreamed of how his lips would feel on hers, but finding out for real had never been a possibility.

How could she say no?

She nodded.

Kallie wasn't sure who moved first – him or her – as she met him halfway across the fence. The people in the ballpark faded into obscurity as their lips clung in a first kiss so right, so *perfect*, that she didn't want it to end. Eventually he drew away. The smattering of applause made blood rush to her face. *I can't believe I just did that in front of so many people!* She glanced around from the corner of her eye. Surprisingly, not many people had paid attention. Just Rafe's teammates, which only increased her discomfort.

"Well, Kallie," Justin said as both she and Rafe regained their composure. "If we don't win tonight, we'll know whose fault it is."

"G-good luck," she stammered, still trying to find her balance as Lucas and Justin continued giving Rafe a hard time.

All three players grinned at her. But it was Lucas who spoke. "Thanks, Kallie."

She nodded, still dazed from the intense connection, then took off toward the concessions on the other side of the stadium, excitement fizzing through her blood.

That was better than she'd dreamt!

What if he doesn't feel the same way? What if he does? Yet her head cautioned her heart to keep from going too far too fast. He could be as big a player off the field as on.

Rafe watched until Kallie disappeared around the bleachers, the feel of her lips lingering on his. He'd been receiving pregame good-luck kisses most of his career, but nothing had prepared him for Kallie. The moment their lips touched, a fire ignited in his gut. Hell, the stadium had melted to nothing, which had never happened before.

Something told him that she was different from the other girls he'd dated. Not that he'd had many girlfriends – only one steady from high school and a very short string of casuals during his first two years of college – but even then, he'd recognized something was off.

His ex, Talia, had kept pushing for commitment, even though he'd made it clear that baseball was his main focus. She hadn't taken too kindly to playing second-fiddle to his dreams, and a screaming match… (mostly from her)…had ended their relationship after their first year of college.

Rafe shook his head, sloughing off the thoughts of his past.

"Dude, that was some serious lip lock," Lucas said as they made their way back toward the bullpen.

"Yeah," Justin agreed. "But you still didn't get her number."

Lucas laughed. "What guy kisses a girl and doesn't get her number?" He formed an L with his thumb and index finger, holding it up to his forehead. "A loser."

"Hey," the first-base coach yelled. "Get your heads in the game!"

"Yes, sir," Justin said, still grinning. To Rafe he said, "Let's go hunt some geese!"

Laughing, Rafe sprinted toward the bullpen and prepared his muscles for nine innings of baseball. He went through the exercises by rote, his mind only half on what he was doing. The other half was on Kallie. He hadn't stopped thinking about her since last night. Their kiss had been better than he'd imagined.

Yet as he continued his pregame ritual to center his focus, he couldn't completely dispel Kallie's image. But he refused to worry whether thoughts of her would throw him off his game.

The concession stand line was backed up to the beer stand on the opposite side of the shelter, and it took forever for Kallie to get her food. She barely made it back to her seat in time to hear the starting lineups.

"Who was that guy you kissed?" Amy asked as Kallie sat back down.

"His name is Rafe." She pointed to where he stood outside the dugout.

"Oh, he's gorgeous!"

Kallie nodded, agreeing wholeheartedly.

Amy waggled her eyebrows. "And he wears his uniform so well."

Kallie blushed, saying nothing as she lifted her sandwich to her lips.

"So…how did you meet him?"

Kallie sighed and set the sandwich back in the paper boat sitting on her lap, mourning the loss of the first bite. "Last night."

Amy's eyes narrowed. "On the Bluff?"

Kallie nodded. "I bumped into him on the way back to my truck after sunset."

Amy didn't let up. "Were you with anyone?"

"No."

Amy stiffened. "Of all the stupid –"

"Ladies and gentlemen, the starting lineups!" The announcer cut Amy's tirade short.

Kallie set her food aside for the pregame festivities as Rochester's players were introduced first, and they all lined up along the first base chalk line. Goose honks cried out again.

"Anyone have a shotgun?" Amy asked, giggling.

Kallie grinned. "Talk about lining them up and knocking them down."

"And now…" the announcer interrupted their giggles, "Your…La Crosse…Loggers!"

The crowd cheered as each player was introduced. Kallie shouted when Rafe's name was called. His uniform pants molded his muscular legs as he ran out onto the field, stopping in shallow center behind second base.

The rest of the team followed. The Coulee Chordsmen, an all-male singing group, sang the National Anthem. Kallie cheered with the crowd when the song ended, and more goose honks rang out. She sat down and finally dug into her food as the pitcher threw the first pitch.

Her sandwich had grown cold.

As Rafe took the field in the top of the first inning, he couldn't help searching the stands for Kallie. He knew she'd be watching, which gave him an unexpected boost of pride. Was she by herself? With friends? Guy friends? Or girlfriends?

The crack from the wooden bat jerked Rafe's thoughts back to the game as the ball sped across the ground toward him.

"Crap!" he muttered and dropped his glove to intercept. Except, the ball rolled right past him into shallow left field. The outfielder scooped it up and threw it to Justin at first. Not in time, but it kept the runner from getting extra bases.

"Come on, Rafe!" Callan hissed from third base. "Get your head in the game. That could have been a double!"

Grimacing, Rafe nodded at his teammate. Yet he couldn't seem to keep his eyes on the field and he ended up scanning the seats again.

Another hit by the opposing team sent a second ball his way, at a much higher speed. Sprinting towards it, he scooped up the ball and set up the throw to second base.

The ball slipped from his fingers and dropped to the ground behind him.

Callan grabbed it and held fast, keeping the runners on first and second, before returning the ball to David on the pitcher's mound.

"Dammit, Rafe!" the second baseman, Brad, scolded. "You should have had that!"

"I'm sorry!" Rafe resisted the urge to throw up his arms in frustration and set his stance for the next play. Silently he promised to do better. The last thing he wanted was to let his teammates and coaches down.

The third batter stepped into the box at home plate.

David threw the next pitches. After a couple that fell outside the strike zone, he finally got one on target.

The hitter connected, sending the ball over the right fielder's head.

Dejected, Rafe hung his head as the runners ran toward home.

His team was already down three to nothing, and it was all his fault.

In the bottom of the second inning the Honkers were up four to nothing, thanks to Rafe missing another throw to first base in what should have been an easy play. Instead, the ball sailed high and wide, allowing another run to score.

During the mid-inning break to allow the sides to switch, Rafe closed his eyes and gave himself a mental shake, pushing all thoughts of Kallie from his head. Grabbing his bat, he gripped either end and bent at the hip flexors, taking a deep breath. Clearing his mind – which wasn't easy to do given the current direction of his thoughts – he focused on the game.

Inhaling, he stood back up and raised the bat above his head, stretching his arms, before lowering the bat back to waist-level.

"Donaldson!" the field manager barked. "You're up!"

Nodding, Rafe jogged toward home plate.

Rafe stepped up to the plate for his first at-bat of the game. Even though the infield was turf, he still drew the initials D and S in the brown "dirt" as a remembrance to his former teammate. Dustin Sanders had been one of his best friends, but he'd passed away from leukemia at the beginning of their senior year in high school. Drawing his initials in the dirt with the knob of his bat before every turn was Rafe's way of keeping his memory alive.

With two outs and bases loaded, Rafe had a chance to tie the game. He set his stance, adjusting his grip on the bat, and waited for his pitch. The first was a curveball strike in the lower right corner. The second pitch a slider strike on the outer left edge. The third was a fastball right down the middle.

Rafe swung…and missed.

The catcher snared the ball with his glove.

Cursing himself for the missed opportunity, he hustled back to the dugout.

He'd screwed up. Big time.

"Where the hell is your head, Donaldson?" the batting coach railed. "With your skills you should have had that fastball."

"I'm sorry, sir." Rafe racked his brain for a plausible excuse, but found none. The coach would be madder if he learned that Kallie's kiss had rattled Rafe more than he cared to admit.

"I suggest you get your head in the game," the coach bellowed, "or yours will be the shortest career on the team."

"Yes, sir." Personally, he felt the ass-chewing was a bit harsh considering it was only the first game of the season, but he had to admit the coach had a point. Kallie's kiss messed with his concentration.

Lucas grabbed his glove. "Tough outing."

"Shut up." Rafe removed his batting helmet, resisting the urge to smash it against the concrete wall as he put on his baseball cap and hustled back onto the field for the next inning. Frustration ate at him, but he couldn't decide if it was from blowing his turn or not being more upset that Kallie made him lose focus on his game. Shaking his head, he pushed her from his thoughts.

The fourth inning went more smoothly than the first three. Two of the three balls hit came toward him, and his throws to first base were on-target and in-time. His teammate Callan Black caught a pop-up in the warning track in foul territory to end the inning.

Rafe sprinted back to the dugout, still distracted by that pre-game kiss.

Justin took his turn at the plate, and sent the ball sailing over the first-baseman's head as it landed just inside the foul line and rolled into the other team's bullpen. The pitchers scattered as the right fielder scrambled to get the ball back in play quickly.

Lucas elbowed Rafe in the ribs. "That's how you get to first base."

The double meaning not lost on him, Rafe ignored him and watched his teammates finish the inning. The fans roared in excitement as Callan hit a line drive to deep right field. The ball dropped between two outfielders and smacked the fence before either player could grab it. Though the right fielder hustled to get the ball back into play, Callan easily beat the tag at third for a triple.

Damn it. Rafe grimaced. *Should've been me.*

Brad laughed. Lucas ribbed him again.

Rafe ignored them both. Standing at the fence, he clapped. "Nice job, Callan!"

Callan waved as he removed his elbow and ankle guards.

Looking around the stands, Rafe thought that opening night was rather quiet. The stands were only about two-thirds full, and all of the party cabins beyond the center field wall were locked up. Mitch, a returning pitcher from last summer, mentioned that usually three thousand Copeland Crazies— as the team from 2008 had dubbed the fans — filled the park for almost every home game. It was still the biggest crowd he'd ever played in front of. Back home he'd normally play in front of a few hundred, made up of mostly his teammates' friends and family.

The game was tied four innings later when Justin took another turn at bat with one out and nobody on base. Rafe watched as Justin swung at the pitch, sending the ball deep into the right-field corner before rolling out of play. Ground-rule double.

Lucas struck out for his turn, and stalked back to the dugout. The coach paid him no heed, making Rafe wonder if it was his kiss with Kallie that prompted the coach's ass-chewing in the second inning.

Rafe caught the tail end of Lucas's grumbles and grinned. "I bet you have as much luck with the ladies as you do with those high, outside fastballs."

"Shut up." Lucas sat next to him. "I'll get 'em next time."

Unfortunately, the next guy grounded out to end the inning. Unless the team got a rally going, Lucas and Justin had probably seen their last at-bats. The eighth inning played out much the same way as the seventh, with the score still tied.

Top of the ninth inning. Two outs, bases juiced. Rafe was loose and fast at the short-stop position, having redeemed himself after his rocky start. The batter hit a line drive right to him, and he snared it in his glove before the ball hit the ground. Out number three. He jogged back to the dugout, high-fiving his teammates as they patted his backside.

Justin grinned. "Lucky stab."

"Wasn't it?" Rafe agreed casually, taking his seat on the bench.

"You probably saved the game with that one."

"Maybe, maybe not." Rafe turned his attention to the field, studying the batter. "Depends on what we can do here."

"Dude." Brad clapped Rafe on the shoulder. "That was a highlight-reel play."

Rafe nodded, his eyes never leaving the field. "Mmm."
As far as he was concerned, he was just doing his job.
Highlight reels were nice, but they weren't his main reason for
playing.

Callan led off the bottom of the ninth. With his turn
coming up. Rafe studied the pitcher, focusing on the other
player's delivery.

"Donaldson," the field manager bellowed at Rafe.
"You're on deck."

Rafe donned his batting helmet and protective guards
then grabbed his bat from where it leaned against the fence,
taking a few practice swings in the on-deck circle near the
dugout.

Strike three. His teammate went down swinging for the
first out. Rafe drew DS in the brown turf then stepped into the
batter's box and set his stance. The first two pitches were
outside the strike zone, so he let them pass. The third was right
down the middle.

He connected. Hard.

The loud *CRACK!* of the wooden bat was music to his
ears. The vibrations shook his arms as he followed through,
then dropped it as he sprinted for first base. The ball climbed
higher as it sailed deep into left-center field. Right over the
fence.

Chapter 3

Kallie leapt to her feet, cheering as Rafe jogged around the bases, touching each one as he passed. When he got back to home plate, the players piled on him.

"You'll have to be at all the home games now," Amy shouted over the roar of the crowd. "That was your boy!"

Kallie blushed, but said nothing as the team tackled Rafe at home plate. When they finally let him up for air, he was still grinning, still high-fiving and chest-bumping. The team lined up and shook hands with the opposing team's players and coaches, then returned to the dugout as the fans filed out of the stands.

"Do you want to hang around?" Amy asked as they started down the stairs.

Kallie wanted to stay and see Rafe, but she had to work early in the morning and she didn't want to look like a groupie. "To be honest, I don't know what I want."

"Let's stick around for a little bit, to see if you can get his attention," Amy said. "After all, it was your kiss that gave him the impetus to win tonight."

Kallie wasn't so sure. He'd had a rocky start to the game with a few throwing errors. She'd caught him looking up into the stands instead of on the field, so she couldn't help but wonder if she'd been the cause. But after the second inning, his gaze never left the area of home plate. *Was he as affected by our kiss as I was?*

Several fans stuck around. One of the traditions that the owners encouraged from the beginning was the post-game on-field autograph session. Fans – mostly kids – filed onto the field to meet and get pictures with the players and coaches. Some dashed into the outfield to play catch, or had fun running the bases. Rafe spent time with the youngsters after he finished with post-game interviews.

Kallie didn't believe in silly superstitions or omens of luck, but she had to admit Amy had a point. She sighed as she dropped her blanket on one of the first-row seats and stood along the rail in an easily-visible spot as her eyes scanned the field. She spotted Rafe almost immediately, as he was a good head taller than his teammates. She took a moment to study him. His deep brown hair glistened beneath the stadium lights as he chatted and signed autographs for the kids. Rafe took the time to answer all the questions asked of him, his smile never wavering.

"He *is* hot," Amy said from beside her. "I'm jealous I didn't meet him first."

Kallie rolled her eyes. "This coming from the woman who scolded me about being on top of the Bluff at dusk by myself."

"If it had been anyone other than him, you'd have been in trouble," Amy said. "But since it was him, I'll forgive you. *This time.*"

Kallie laughed. "You're so generous."

"I try to be. Now, go on that field and get your hunk." Amy nudged her toward the stairs.

Kallie wasn't expecting the shove, and almost landed on her butt. Grabbing the handrail, she caught herself before she fell. Up to that point, Rafe had kept his attention on the kids. One of his teammates said something to him, and he looked up. Her gaze locked with his across the distance. His smile grew and he nodded. Kallie smiled back. It was all she could do. Her feet were suddenly welded to the bleachers.

Rafe extricated himself from the legion of fans surrounding him and made a beeline straight for her, taking the stairs two at a time. He took her in his arms and kissed her. "Hey, beautiful."

Kallie grasped his firm forearms, needing something solid to hold onto while she regained her bearings. Her lashes fluttered open. "Hi."

"Congrats on the homer," Amy said. "I'm Amy, Kallie's best friend."

"Nice to meet you, Amy." Turning, Rafe accepted her handshake.

"Likewise." Amy smiled.

They heard hooting and hollering from the field. Kallie, still recovering from the overwhelming power of Rafe's kiss, turned her head in the direction of the ruckus. Justin and Lucas waved at her. She waved back as heat crept up her face.

"Hey, Rafe!" Justin yelled. "You gonna get her number this time?"

Groaning softly, Kallie buried her face in Rafe's throat. The scent of post-game athlete invaded her senses. All sweaty and earthy and elemental. And something pure Rafe. She could taste the salt tang of his skin beneath her lips. She was instantly intoxicated, and wanted more.

"What do you say, Kallie?" he whispered in her ear. "Can I call you?"

The way he said her name made her stomach flip. "I – I'd like that."

"Wait around just a little bit longer. Let me talk to the kids some more, then we'll exchange numbers."

She straightened, nodding. Rafe kissed her once more, on the forehead this time, before joining the rest of the team back on the field.

Amy fanned herself with her program. "Damn, he's hot."

Kallie laughed. "I believe we've already established that."

"Yeah, well, it bears repeating." Amy chuckled. "I'm still jealous you met him first."

"I'm sure he could hook you up with one of his teammates." Kallie leaned against the top of the rail. "You're prettier than I am. It won't be difficult."

"Maybe I am, maybe I'm not," Amy teased, scanning the field. "Hmm. Lucas is nice. Not as good-looking as Rafe, but I'm willing to settle for second-best."

Kallie looked out over the field again, remembering the last time she and Amy had been interested in the same guy. They'd been juniors in high school. The guy had been more interested in Amy, so Kallie had stepped aside. No boy was worth risking their friendship over. It turned out for the best, though, because the guy had turned into a world-class jackass. He'd dumped Amy because she wouldn't have sex with him after Prom.

"Earth to Kallie," Amy tapped her shoulder.

"What?" Kallie absently worried her bottom lip with her teeth.

"Have you heard anything I said?"

Kallie blushed again.

"I'll take that as a no. I'll let you get away with it for now." Amy chuckled, wrapping her arm around Kallie's shoulder. "Remember to name your first kid after me."

Before Kallie could respond, most of the players left and Rafe gestured her to join him on the field. Dumping their stuff onto the first row of bleachers near the fence, she and Amy headed for the dugout gate. As Kallie was about to join him, an older woman appeared from the fray and gave him a hug. Kallie hesitated.

Amy shoved her from behind. "Get going!"

Kallie joined Rafe on the artificial turf. He draped his arm over her shoulder, the heavy weight comforting, as he introduced the matronly woman with smiling blue eyes and salt-and-pepper curls.

"Sue, I'd like you to meet Kallie. Kallie, this is my host mom, Sue Carmichael."

Kallie offered her hand. "Nice to meet you, Mrs. Carmichael."

"Call me Sue, dear," she replied, accepting the handshake. "It's nice to meet you. This is my husband, Ed." She gestured to the tall, bespectacled man standing next to her.

"Nice to meet you both as well," Kallie replied, not knowing what else to say.

"Grab your stuff, dear," Sue said to Rafe. "Ed and I will take it home so you can spend time with the guys."

"Thanks, Sue." He turned to Kallie. "Want to join us? We're going for pizza."

Kallie looked at her watch. As much as she wanted to … "I better not. I have to work in the morning."

"What time?" Rafe didn't give up.

"Eight."

"Till when?"

"Four-thirty."

"Hey, Rafe." Lucas called out, interrupting them. "You comin' or not, bro?"

"Yeah, I'll be there in a sec," he replied.

"You better go," Kallie said, turning to leave. "Enjoy the rest of your night."

"Uh-uh, Kallie." Rafe wrapped his arms around her waist from behind and pressed his lips to the sensitive spot at the nape of her neck. "Not so fast. You agreed to exchange numbers, remember?"

Fighting the desire from his touch igniting inside her, Kallie laughed. "Well, since you put it that way…"

Rafe kissed the side of her neck, then let her go. He grabbed his phone, wallet and keys from his black bat bag before handing it to Ed. He keyed in her phone number, then immediately sent her a text to give her his.

"Don't stay out too late," Ed admonished. "You have another game tomorrow."

"Yes, sir." Rafe turned to Kallie, giving her another hug. "Thanks, Kallie. I'll call you."

"Okay." She nodded. "Enjoy your night." Kallie left the field and grabbed her stuff, her thoughts floating on a cloud.

Rafe, Justin and Lucas piled into Rafe's car.

"Dude, I can't believe you didn't ask her out." Justin snapped his seatbelt into place.

"I did." Rafe started the car and pulled out of the parking lot. "She has to work tomorrow."

Lucas grinned. "She shot you down."

"No, she didn't," Rafe replied, turning onto Copeland Avenue heading toward the pizzeria downtown. "I got her phone number."

"'Bout damn time. You've been going on about her since last night."

"See? I'm not as dumb as you look," Rafe taunted.

"If you were real smart," Justin said, "you'd have gotten her number right away."

"Shut up." Rafe turned into the parking ramp a block from the restaurant. "Unless you feel like walking home."

David joined them shortly after they found a table.

"That was some awesome swinging." Lucas sat next to Rafe. "Did you do it for her?"

Rafe rolled his eyes. "I liked the pitch, so I swung."

"Uh-huh." Lucas shifted in his seat.

"Fine. Don't believe me." Rafe glared at him. "But I got mine before you got yours."

Lucas chuckled. "I bet it didn't hurt that she was watching, did it?"

Rafe rolled his eyes, elbowing Lucas lightly in his ribs. Then he grinned. "No," he said at last. "It didn't."

The three hours spent unwinding at the pizza joint were some of the best of Rafe's brief season. He and his three teammates might have come from different colleges, but for now they all played on the same squad. They talked about their dreams of landing a spot on a professional baseball roster, and about how none of them had taken the process for granted.

Though Rafe had expected more comments, none of his new friends teased him again about Kallie. Though she was never far from his thoughts.

"Are there any decent clubs in this town?" Rafe asked aloud.

"No clue," Justin said. "But Rafe, you don't want your first date to involve loud, thumping music."

"I agree." Lucas stabbed a chunk of spicy Italian sausage with his fork and popped it into his mouth. "You should take her someplace quiet. Where you can talk."

Rafe silently agreed. For the first time in as long as he could remember, a woman shifted his focus away from baseball.

He met Kallie only twenty-four hours ago, but something pulled inside him, making him *want* to pursue a relationship with her. To see where they could go.

But can he hold onto Kallie with one hand and his dreams with the other, without losing his grasp on both?

Chapter 4

Rafe hurried down the steps of his host-family's house and headed for the car as Lucas honked the horn of his borrowed sedan. "Hurry up, dude!"

"Hold your horses!" Rafe hollered back, grinning.

He had hoped to spend the day with Kallie because it was his first day off since the season started three weeks ago, but she hadn't been able to get the day off of work. Frustration eroded his patience as each attempt at planning their first official date had failed. His game schedule and her job kept getting in the way, and he had a feeling the clock was ticking against them.

That morning's practice at the Lumberyard had gone well, and Rafe was ready for a break. "I gotta stop at the pet store for a bag of dog food." He slid into the car. "Sassy's almost out."

"Sassy?" Lucas laughed.

"Sue's frou-frou toy poodle," he said, referring to his host-mom.

Lucas pulled away from the curb and headed toward the north side of La Crosse. "Dang, whoever came up with the layout of these streets is messed up," he exclaimed, turning left onto a side street that led toward the small amusement park. "If I didn't have sat nav on my dash, I'd have no clue where I'm going."

"They're not as bad as Dallas," Rafe countered.

Lucas pulled into the parking lot and killed the motor. "No place is as bad as Dallas," he agreed.

Rafe laughed. Lucas attended Sacramento City Community College, which had one of the top-notch baseball programs in California.

"What do you want to do first?" Lucas asked as they entered Riverside Amusement Park and scoped out the available attractions.

"I dunno. Wanna try the go-karts?"

They took a moment to watch the racers currently driving around the looped track.

"Yeah. Those look like fun." Lucas turned. "How about mini golf?"

"Nah." Rafe shook his head. "Too tame. There aren't enough obstacles on it." Rafe thought about the putting course back home, with windmills, water hazards and other moving obstacles. Now that was a challenge. He gazed around the golf course. From his perspective, the only things it had going for it were several water hazards and a fountain at the top. "I've got my eye on the batting cages." He shrugged. "Might as well get some extra practice in while we get the chance. Right?"

"Not that you need it." Lucas snickered. "Your batting average is still up over four hundred."

"Well, with yours tankin' at one seventy-five, you could use it," Rafe taunted. Ignoring Lucas's glare, Rafe clapped him on the shoulder. "Let's have some fun."

The boys went to the window and paid for a round at the cages, then headed for the gear and waited their turn.

"Any news from your girl yet?" Lucas asked.

"My girl?" Rafe looked at his teammate, feigning confusion.

Lucas laughed. "Yeah. Your good-luck charm from the first game."

"Oh." Heat scalded the tips of Rafe's ears, a sure sign he was blushing. "We've talked a couple times over the phone, and she's been to a few more games, but we haven't gone out on any dates yet."

"What are you waiting for, boy?" Lucas palmed his bat in a crude sexual gesture. "If you don't want her, I'll take her."

Rafe saw red, but he calmed himself before he took a swing at his teammate. "Leave her alone."

Realization dawned on Lucas's face. "You really like her."

Rafe shrugged. As much as he'd tried, he couldn't be casual about her. He was honest enough to admit to himself that, despite having only spent a short amount of time with Kallie, his heart was already involved.

Which was ridiculous, right? He leaned against the side of the building. How could he have fallen for a woman after only a few weeks?

One thing he had noticed was that his on-field performance was better when Kallie wasn't at his games.

Can I have a girlfriend and baseball at the same time? Is that what I want?

Before he had a chance to ponder further, Lucas nudged him out of his reverie.

The kids in the two fast-pitch baseball cages finished up their rounds and exited the enclosed area. Rafe picked up his bat and stepped inside the chain-linked batter's box, inserting his token into the slot for the mechanical pitching arm. Lucas did the same in the next cage over.

Figures, he thought, waiting for the red light to flash. Rafe batted right-handed, while Lucas batted left-handed. Their juxtaposition had them facing each other.

As the first pitch flung toward him at eighty miles per hour, he imagined his teammate's face on the ball. He swung, and connected with the barrel of the bat. The ball careened through the netted cage, all the way to the other side.

The next pitch came at him a few seconds later. Rafe reset and sent the second ball trailing after the first. Out of the corner of his eye, he watched his friend miss his second swing, before turning his eye back to his pitching arm and connecting with the next. And the next.

Five minutes later they stepped out of the cages and removed their protective helmets.

"How did you do?" Lucas asked.

"Hit them all. You?"

"About one of three."

"Dude, you suck!" Rafe taunted him. "Told ya you needed the extra practice."

Lucas slugged Rafe's catching arm. "Shut up. Let's hit the go-karts."

They showed their IDs to the attendant and paid for their rides. They were in line for the Bombers when Rafe heard a voice behind him.

"You're Rafe Donaldson and Lucas McCormick, right?"

Rafe turned to the little boy on the other side of the low fence and smiled. "Yeah, we are." He shook the kid's hand, taking in the shabby-looking clothing. Something tugged at Rafe's heart. Most of his clothing growing up had been second-hand thrift-store finds because that was all his mother could afford.

"Dude, you're, like, the best!" the kid gushed.

Lucas laughed.

Rafe grinned. "I think some of my teammates would disagree with you."

"No way!" the kid exclaimed. "They're all just jealous of you."

"Thanks." Rafe didn't know what to say. This little boy's high praise caught him off guard. Remembering how he'd felt every time a ball player had spent any time talking to him, he asked, "How about an autograph?"

"Sure!"

Lucas slugged his arm. "We're up, dude."

"Can you wait here until I get done? I don't know how long we'll be on the track," Rafe said to the boy. "I'll sign something for you afterwards."

"Yeah!" The boy nodded enthusiastically.

Rafe ruffled the little boy's hair then weaved his way through the fence and picked out his kart. He buckled himself in and leaned back, waiting for the signal from the attendant. Punching the gas, he peeled out of the starting line and drove onto the track.

Ten minutes later Rafe drove into the lane, parked his ride and climbed out. The kid was still waiting by the fence, but a young woman had joined him. He held out his hand to her, learning that she was his older sister.

"How do tickets to a game sound?" he asked.

The little boy beamed. "That would be awesome!"

His sister smoothed his hair. "It depends on the night. Mom's and my work schedules are kind of erratic."

The young boy's face fell a bit.

"What about tomorrow night?" Rafe asked.

She dug a cell phone from her pocket. "Let me call our parents."

While she was on the phone, Rafe went to the concessions counter and signed a piece of scrap paper. Lucas signed it as well, and Rafe handed it to the boy as his sister disconnected the call.

"Mom says tomorrow's fine." She put her hand on her brother's shoulder.

"Great." Rafe grabbed his cell phone. After getting their names, he called the team's general manager. He turned back to the girl when he'd hung up. "You're all set. Give your names to the guy at the ticket counter at the field."

"Thanks, Rafe!" The boy wrapped his arms tight around Rafe's waist.

Not prepared for the impact, he stumbled back a step and laughed. "You're welcome."

The kid hugged Lucas, though with not as much enthusiasm.

"Thank you again," the sister said, smiling. "He loves baseball, but we aren't able to get to many games."

"My pleasure." Rafe shook her hand again. "See you tomorrow night."

Rafe grabbed Lucas' shirtsleeve as they headed back to the car. "We need to make one more stop on our way home. I need Sassy's food."

They climbed into the sedan and Lucas started the ignition. "Where do you want to go?"

"The pet store by the mall. They're the only place that carries the right brand."

"Dude, seriously? Sue named a toy poodle 'Sassy?' That's like naming a grizzly bear 'Fluffy!'"

Rafe rolled his eyes. "Just go."

Ten minutes later they pulled into the parking lot of the store and headed inside.

"Dude, this place is like an amusement park for Fido," Lucas commented. "Zeus would have a field day in here."

"Zeus?" Rafe asked.

"My parents' German shepherd." Lucas looked around. "Let's get that fancy mutt's food and get back to the house."

Rafe chuckled. "Sounds good to me."

Though he wouldn't call the dog a mutt. Sassy was purebred through and through.

They were walking down the food aisles looking for poodle kibble when they ended up near the salon at the back of the store.

"Dude, ain't that your girl?" Lucas asked, pointing.

"Yeah, it is." Rafe recognized her immediately in the mirror spanning the entire length of the back wall. He stood there, entranced, watching her brush out the golden retriever on her table, until their gazes connected in the mirror. She smiled as she continued combing the dog's fur.

"Wow." Lucas gave a low whistle. "She's hot."

Rafe's mental capabilities flew out the window as he imagined those delicate hands working him. He didn't realize Lucas was still talking to him until he snapped his fingers in front of Rafe's nose.

"Earth to Rafe," Lucas teased.

Rafe jumped guiltily.

"Let's get the food," Lucas said. "We're going out tonight."

Rafe didn't budge when Lucas tugged his arm. He could only watch Kallie brush the dog, until she finally slipped a leash around the animal's neck and guided it into the back. She returned moments later, empty-handed. She said something to her co-workers as she headed for the salon entrance. Right for him.

When Kallie saw Rafe in the store, she almost lost her grip on the metal greyhound comb as she finished brushing Bruno's silky, red-gold coat. He hadn't been far from her thoughts. She'd gone to more games and they'd talked on the phone when his schedule had permitted, but they still hadn't been on a 'real' date. After she'd returned the dog to the kennel, she told the salon manager that she was stepping out for a moment. Grabbing her water bottle, she headed for the door.

"Hey, beautiful," Rafe greeted her with a hug.

"Hey, yourself." She smiled, returning his embrace. "Hi, Lucas."

"Kallie." Lucas nodded. "You comin' to the game tomorrow night? I'm sure the boy here could use some more of whatever you gave him last time."

Kallie blushed, remembering the pregame kiss they'd shared the day after he'd bumped into her on top of the bluff.

"Please?" Rafe asked. "They've got fireworks tomorrow."

Because she was interested in seeing where she and Rafe were headed, she twined her fingers behind his neck and pressed against his side. "What girl could refuse that offer?"

He rested his hands lightly on her hips. "It's a date, darlin'."

She nodded. "Yeah, I guess it is."

He kissed her, just a soft brush of his lips against hers, but it made her knees turn to jelly. A tap on the glass forced her to quickly back up out of his embrace.

Turning, she glanced into the salon, to see her coworkers applauding her.

Blushing, she shoved her hands into the pockets of her smock and looked back at Rafe and Lucas. "I better get back to work. I have another dog waiting for a haircut."

"I'll see you tomorrow then." Rafe scratched behind his ear. "Can I call you later?"

"I'm going out with Amy tonight, but I can text you when I get home."

Something flashed in Rafe's eyes when Kallie mentioned her friend, but it was gone before she could interpret it. A sliver of unease skated down her spine, for the first time since she'd bumped into him on the bluff.

She seriously hoped he wasn't one of those guys who were possessive over their girlfriends. Because *that* would be a deal-breaker.

Chapter 5

Kallie stood at the fence separating the field from the stands, watching as Rafe and his teammates went through their pregame warm-up drills. One of his teammates – David? – tapped him on the shoulder and pointed in her direction. She smiled as her gaze connected with Rafe's across the field. He jogged over to her when he finished stretching.

"Hey, beautiful." He cupped her cheek in his warm, calloused palm.

She leaned into his touch. "Hey."

"Gonna give me a kiss for luck again tonight?" His green eyes danced with laughter.

Kallie pulled back, but not enough to break contact. "Maybe, maybe not," she teased.

"Well, I might have to steal one anyway," he said in the same light tone.

"Aren't stolen kisses bad luck?"

His grin was as brilliant as the early-evening sun. "Darlin', any kiss from you is good luck."

"In that case, I might as well save you the trouble." Their lips met across the fence. Light at first, but quickly transforming into spectacular passion. They were both panting when they parted. Her heart pounded. "Good luck," was all she could whisper.

"Count on it." Rafe caressed her cheek again. "Meet me here after the game?"

Kallie nodded, her heart racing from the desire flowing through her body as she watched Rafe jog back to where the rest of the team was still going through warmup drills.

She returned to her seat next to Amy, who was busy munching on a walking taco.

"Didja kiss him?" she asked between bites.

"How could I not have?" Kallie replied, blushing. "He's the best kisser I've had in a long time."

Amy finished her meal and crumpled the wrapper, then stuck it beneath the bench seat. "That goes without saying. Didn't the last guy have fish lips or something?"

Kallie cringed at the memory. "Something like that."

In the bottom of the second inning, Amy dug her phone from her purse and snapped several photos of the Loggers player at the plate waiting for the pitch.

His uniform hugged his thighs and calves like a second skin, accentuating every line and curve of his legs and backside.

"Damn, he's hot," Amy said, scrolling through the shots.

"Just don't ogle Rafe like that," Kallie warned. "I might have to unleash my inner green-eyed monster."

"As if I would!" Amy guffawed. She turned the camera lens back to home plate.

"Just sayin'." Kallie glanced out over the field.

Rafe stepped into the batter's box and set his stance. He batted left-handed, so he faced her side of the bleachers when he took his turn at the plate.

Amy zoomed in and snapped another photo, then angled the phone toward Kallie.

Kallie saw the intense concentration etched into every line of his face, from the firm set of his jaw to the way his eyebrows flattened beneath his batting helmet.

He swung at the pitch, his muscles bunching and flexing as his bat connected with the ball, the loud *CRACK!* echoing through the early-evening air.

The ball sailed deep into center field, dropping just enough to hit the top of the wall without going over.

Standing, Kallie cheered for Rafe as he ran the bases at full speed, finally stopping at third for the triple.

Admittedly she didn't know enough to distinguish between a fastball, curveball and slider, but she saw how quickly the ball traveled between the pitcher's hand and the catcher's mitt.

Another batter stepped into the box, his back to them, and Amy snapped a couple more photos. Backsides only, of course. "Yummy," she murmured.

Kallie giggled. "You're such a floozy."

"Takes one to know one." Amy stuck out her tongue.

"You would know." Kallie fell into their familiar banter. Though if she were honest with herself, her relationship with Rafe made her feel more like an adult than anything she'd done before, including college. "Go, Rafe!"

The noise level of the stadium was so loud she doubted he heard her, though she was only six rows up from the dugout along the third-base line. He didn't look up, which made her heart clench painfully.

Rafe had a good game, as did the rest of his teammates. They beat St. Cloud, whom they'd been struggling against all summer, by five-nothing. Rafe went three-for-four, including a two-run homer that sailed over the fence and slammed into a car parked along Copeland Avenue.

Kallie hoped the owner wasn't too mad about the damage. Smashed windows were one of the hazards of parking near a baseball park on game-day. As soon as the game ended Kallie went to meet Rafe, but Security stopped her at the gate. She still had a view of the team in the dugout. Rafe was in the process of changing out of his uniform. She took great joy in watching him towel off and had to fan herself after he finished.

"It's okay, Matt." Rafe joined them at the gate. "She's with me."

Matt guided her through as the announcer started the countdown to lights-out. Kallie inhaled the scent that clung to his skin as she and Rafe got comfortable on the grass. Moments later, the stadium plunged into darkness and the first rockets exploded across the sky in a glitter of color.

"Thanks for comin'," Rafe said.

"Thank you for inviting me." She snuggled closer. "Great game."

Rafe was wearing a gray Loggers t-shirt and black shorts, his skin still damp with sweat. He was so close his breath whispered across the sensitive shell of her ear. He put his arm around her shoulder, and the warmth emanating from him seeped into her skin. She shivered.

"Cold?" he asked.

Kallie smiled. "Not anymore."

Rafe chuckled. His fingers lightly clasped her chin, turning her to face him. He brushed his lips across hers. Fireworks exploded again, both in the air and behind her closed eyelids as he deepened the kiss.

Kallie leaned against Rafe as brilliant colors burst across the sky. She inhaled, the salty tang of his sweat teasing her senses. So did something more elemental. Something pure Rafe.

As spectacular as the finale was, Kallie didn't want the fireworks to end. Rafe pulled away shortly after the last of the glittering sparks died. The loss of warmth was an acute physical pain. They both stood, and he guided her back to the gate.

"Do you have to be back right away?" he asked. "I've been trying to take you out on a date for a while, but the timing never worked."

Kallie smiled, shaking her head. "I'd love nothing more."

Rafe pressed a gentle kiss to her cheek, then went back into the dugout and gathered his stuff. He passed his bag to Ed, who stood nearby.

"Don't be out too late," Ed admonished Rafe. "You have another game tomorrow."

"Yes, sir," Rafe said respectfully, shaking the man's hand. His host parent passed him a set of keys, and he turned back to Kallie. "Ready?"

Kallie nodded, smiling as he wrapped his arm around her waist and guided her out to the car. He held open the door for her as she got in, then closed it with care as she buckled her seatbelt.

Grimacing, he slid behind the wheel and turned the key in the ignition. "I'm sorry I'm not dressed nicer for our first date."

Kallie shrugged. "It's not – I don't –" She broke off, sighing, not sure how she should put her thoughts into words. "I'm not expecting anything fancy," she said at last.

He drove out of the parking lot and into traffic. "But you were expectin' more."

"I wasn't." She rested her hand on his thigh and was about to explain, but the words died on her tongue as she became aware of the shift in atmosphere inside the car. The silky fabric of his shorts was soft beneath her touch, and she curled her fingers lightly into the corded muscle of his thigh. He jumped, the tremors tickling her palm. Her stomach flipped and she snatched her hand back. "I'm sorry."

He chuckled, the sound skating across her nerves. "Why did you move your hand?"

"I – I shouldn't have –"

"I don't mind."

Her mouth ran dry and the air hitched in her lungs. Kallie gulped, unable to formulate a coherent thought. Did she dare touch him again? He said he didn't mind, but he didn't say to put her hand back where it was.

Instead, she knotted her fingers into her lap and turned her head to look out the window.

Ten minutes later Rafe pulled into the parking lot of a family-style café.

"This place is one of my favorites," Kallie said as they exited the car.

Rafe escorted her to the door, his hand on her back. Heat from his hand seeped through her shirt as the waitress showed them to their table.

"Thank you," Kallie said to the waitress as she slid into the booth. Instead of sitting across from her, Rafe slid onto the bench next to her. "What –"

He caressed her cheek. "I can't be with you and not touch you."

"I like it when you touch me." Butterflies danced in her stomach as she met his gaze.

"I do, too, darlin'." He grinned. "But I like it more when you touch back."

She leaned her head on his shoulder. His lips met her temple, and her pulse kicked up the tempo as desire spread through her body. Despite not being at the right time in her life to start a relationship, she knew her heart would ache if she never saw him again after he went back home.

"What do you recommend?" he asked, flipping open the menu.

"Everything," she said, "but my favorite is the chocolate chip pancakes."

"Sounds interestin'. Sourdough or buttermilk?"

"Buttermilk."

"Have you tried sourdough flapjacks?" Rafe's Texas drawl was more pronounced.

Kallie turned to face him. "N – no," she stammered, losing herself in his deep green eyes that she almost missed the question. "I can't say that I have."

Rafe grinned, one corner of his lips kicking up higher than the other. "Nothin' beats sourdough pancakes cooked over an open campfire."

The passion in his eyes ignited a matching response within her. "I – I'll take your word."

The waitress stopped by their table, breaking the spell Rafe had woven around Kallie.

"Good evening," she said, placing two glasses of water on the table. "What can I get for you?"

Kallie was still too caught up to speak, but Rafe ordered for them both. She roused from the spell long enough to request chips only on the tops of each cake.

"So, Kallie," Rafe said when the woman left. "Tell me about you."

"There isn't much to tell," she said. "I'm twenty-one, and I'm working my way through school."

"Sounds familiar. What's your major?"

"Clinical Laboratory Science."

"What made you choose that?" he asked.

Kallie shrugged. "My uncle passed away from non-Hodgkin's Lymphoma my senior year of high school. I was so frustrated from watching cancer leech his life that I decided to join the fight. My ultimate goal is to get into a research laboratory where I can help find cures for cancers and other chronic diseases."

"That's noble." He pushed a stray clump of hair behind her ear. "I'm sorry for your loss."

"Thank you." She shivered from the contact and changed the subject. "What's your major?"

"Business Administration."

She did a double-take. "Wow. Not what I expected."

"What did you think?" He sipped his water.

She sat back, considering her answer. "I don't know. Something with sports."

"Yeah, I get that a lot. But Dallas Baptist has an amazing BA program. I want somethin' to fall back on if I don't make it to the majors."

She nodded, impressed. "Most college guys don't have as grounded an outlook as yours."

His smile faded a bit. "Most college guys didn't –."

He broke off with a shake of his head. She waited a few beats for him to continue, but he didn't.

"What happened?" she asked in the lengthening silence. Rafe was quiet so long she regretted bringing up the subject. "You don't have to –"

"It's okay. I want to." Rafe grazed his thumb across her lower lip. "My dad left my mom when she was pregnant with me. He never came back, and I never found out who he was."

Kallie's heart twisted from the sadness in his eyes, and she laid her hand against his stubbled cheek. "I'm sorry."

He shook his head. "It's not your fault, darlin'. It's hard sometimes, but Mom and I survived. She works two jobs to keep food on the table and a roof over our heads. I can't wait for the day that I can support her so she can quit workin' so hard."

"I don't blame you. I sometimes forget how fortunate I am." She still had both parents and her sister, and their house was almost always bursting with love. "Do you have any other family?"

He shook his head. "It's me and my mom. I'm hopin' that, since I'm in college, she'll find a nice man who'll love her the way she deserves." He took a breath, held it, then exhaled on a sigh. "What about you, Kallie? Any other family?"

"One sister, two years younger. She's one of my best friends."

"I would've liked havin' a brother, but it would've been too difficult for Mom."

"I bet." She reached for her ice water, taking a long drink. Emotion charged the air between them.

"I had a hard upbringin', Kallie," he said, his voice suddenly rough. "I won't deny that it's defined me in a way, but I'm determined to not let it control me. I'm workin' damn hard to make sure my mom enjoys the rest of her life."

Kallie met his gaze, gasping at the desire she saw there. She suddenly saw herself falling in love with this Texan ballplayer. He was a strong, dependable, handsome guy about to start the prime of his life. But telling him so wouldn't be fair to either of them. She was determined to enjoy whatever time they had together. "I hope you make it," she said instead. "You've got incredible talent on the field."

"Scouts said the same thing." Rafe grinned. "Baseball won't be the same without you there to cheer me on. I'll miss your good-luck kisses when I go back to Texas."

Kallie's heart wedged into her throat, choking the breath from her lungs.

Rafe regretted the words as soon as he'd spoken them. He kissed her temple. "I'm sorry."

Kallie shook her head. "No, it – I get it. You're only here for the summer."

"I never expected to meet someone who –" he broke off. Saying the words would make them real, and he wasn't ready for that step.

His words hung in the air as the waitress brought their food. His heart thumped. Kallie was the first woman he'd met who could make him think of giving up his dreams. He knew it made him sound a bit shallow, but he was almost grateful when their waitress appeared.

"This looks amazin'." Rafe's mouth watered as he buttered the stack on his plate and poured maple syrup over them, ready to savor the first bite of chocolate mixed with fluffy flapjack. Instead, he found himself watching as she did the same. The moan she made in the back of her throat had him reacting in a purely male way, drawing attention to his baser appetites. He focused on his plate, doing his best to ignore the bead of sweat sliding between his shoulder blades.

"My number-one favorite comfort food," she commented between bites. "Daddy used to make these for my sister and me all the time."

Rafe enjoyed eating his meal almost as much as he enjoyed watching her. Her unusual eyes captivated him. Violet blue, like his mom's favorite actress Elizabeth Taylor. More violet than blue, almost the color of amethyst. And they seemed to sparkle every time she smiled or laughed.

He had to admit he'd had his doubts about how well maple, chocolate and buttermilk pancake would fit together, but his first bite quickly dispelled them. "I see why. My mom will love these."

"What's your favorite comfort food?" She brought another forkful to her lips.

"Right now, it's this." Rafe held up his next bite as his gaze followed the movement of her fork from the plate to her mouth. A smear of chocolate appeared on the corner of her upper lip.

He kissed her, unable to resist swiping his tongue over that smudge. Pancakes, chocolate, maple, and Kallie. The combination was so addicting that he almost forgot they were in a restaurant. He leaned back against the seat and furrowed his brow.

Worry clouded her eyes. "Is everything all right?"

Keep it light, he reminded himself. *She doesn't need to know you're falling for her.* He nodded, clearing his throat. "Yeah." He cut another wedge from the stack on his own plate and ate it, chewing slowly as the thoughts swirled around in his brain. He swallowed. "What's your favorite type of music?"

"I like all kinds." Her head cocked to the side. "Except hip-hop and rap."

He shuddered. "I feel the same way. Rap's not music. It's noise pollution."

"Let me guess." She chuckled. "Being from Texas, you like country."

He laughed with her. "Yeah, I do. But don't get me confused with cowboys. I don't rope, and I don't ride."

"I ride," she said. "But I don't rope, either."

His eyebrow quirked as he ate another bite. "There are places to ride in this town?"

"A few, mainly on the outskirts." A teasing glint made her eyes sparkle like amethysts. Such an unusual color. "The city doesn't stretch forever."

He gave her a slow, lazy smile. "Maybe you can take me ridin' sometime."

One corner of her lips kicked up. "I'd like that." She took another bite of her dinner. "You'll have to let me know what works for you. With your crazy schedule and all."

"I think that can be arranged." A strong emotion flooded him, but he didn't dare name it.

"When do you go back to school?" she asked.

Rafe cleared his throat, resisting the urge to shift in his seat. Her innocuous question drove home how temporary their situation was, more than anything else could. "Right after the season ends."

He couldn't afford to stay longer, even bunking with the Carmichaels. Suddenly he wished he didn't have to get back right away. He would've loved to spend a week with her afterwards.

Rafe took her home after their late supper. On the way back to the Carmichaels' house he couldn't remember when he'd done so little on a date but had more fun. Kallie was smart, funny, sassy, and sweet. He loved getting to know her.

Would she consider moving to Texas after the summer? The thought hit him in the gut from left field. *Or maybe come with me if I sign with the Rangers?*

Rafe entered the house and went to the basement bedroom he shared with Callan. Both Rafe and Kallie were starting their last year of college, and their career paths couldn't be more divergent if they'd tried. His dream was to play professional baseball. His end goal was to play for Texas so he could be close to his mom, but the odds weren't in his favor. The chances of him making it to the majors were between slim and none as it was. And if he was cut or traded in the minors, he'd have to start over. *It wouldn't be fair to either of us.*

Rafe changed for bed and climbed beneath the thin blanket. He knew he had to make it that far first, before he could make it up to the majors. At twenty-one, he had his whole life ahead of him. He couldn't afford the distraction of settling down. But damn if the thought of never seeing Kallie again didn't feel like a dagger through the heart.

Chapter 6

Rafe slid the motel keycard into the slot and opened the door. Crossing the room, he tossed his duffel at the foot of the bed by the window. He'd been selected, along with Lucas and Callan, to represent the Loggers at the All-Star game. He glanced outside, not really seeing the scenery as he recalled the last conversation he'd had with Kallie.

He and Kallie had been dating for six weeks, but between his games and her work schedule they hadn't gone out again. Their too-short phone conversations always left him wanting more.

A loud thud caught his attention, and he turned. Lucas flipped him the bird as he dropped his bags at the foot of the other bed. "What makes you think you get the window?"

Rafe chuckled. "First come, first serve."

"Whatever, dude." Lucas grabbed his shampoo and disappeared into the bathroom, closing the door behind him. Moments later water started running.

Lucas apparently didn't want the window too badly. He'd barely kicked up a fuss.

Rafe turned back to the scenery, his thoughts again returning to Kallie. Who was he kidding? Her image had become a permanent fixture in his mind.

He'd asked Kallie to go with him for support, but she'd said no. He hadn't realized how badly he wanted her there until she'd declined. But he respected her decision, and didn't beg. When they'd talked yesterday, he'd suggested not playing so they could spend the three-day break together. She'd immediately shot the idea down, reminding him that he'd be performing in front of professional scouts, and that if he wanted the best shot at the majors, he had to go. He couldn't fault her logic, but her rejection still hurt.

Rafe unpacked the meager things he brought with him and changed into his dress suit for All Star Orientation.

Three hours later, he and Lucas returned to their motel room, Rafe's thoughts still spinning from the massive amounts of information that had just been crammed into his brain.

"Face it, man." Lucas tossed his wallet into his duffel. "She's priming you for a life in the minors. We both know it isn't easy, and the road is no way to start a new marriage."

"Hell, Lucas." Rafe cut him off. "I know that! I'm not lookin' for a wife."

"Regardless, long-distance relationships are hard. My roommate at Sac City is still struggling to make it work with his fiancée."

Rafe plopped down on the bed and shoved his fingers through his hair. "Tell me somethin' I don't know." He couldn't keep the bitterness from his voice.

The mattress dipped as Lucas sat next to him on the bed.

"Rafe," he said softly, "are you in love with Kallie?"

Rafe's heart thumped. "That's impossible."

Right?

Rafe still wasn't sure how he did it, but he'd pushed Kallie out of his mind the last two days as he showed the scouts what he could do, proving he deserved a shot at a professional contract. The Northwoods League North division won the All-Star game, and he gave his personal best performance of the season.

He returned to La Crosse with mixed emotions. He should be flying high. Kallie had been right. Several scouts had said he showed promise on the field. A couple said they'd be in touch. He should have been on top of the world. But not being able to share the experience with her dampened his excitement. The All-Star break marked the halfway point through the second half of the season. Two weeks to go. Two weeks left with Kallie.

Well. He kicked off his shoes and plopped on the bed at his borrowed La Crosse residence. *At least I can still keep my head in the game.* Though he'd had his doubts after his blunders the night he'd met Kallie.

Adding insult to injury, the team started on the road when regular play resumed. Six games in five days. The days in Wisconsin and Minnesota were hotter than blazes. Rafe was used to triple-digit temps back home, but there the air was dry.

Their first game back in La Crosse, with the humidity, felt like a hundred. Even at game time, the air was still scorching. And the bugs! The insects flying around the stadium lights were so dense they looked like snowflakes.

He watched one land on Lucas' back. It looked like a long mealworm, with wings and antennae. "Ew." He swatted it away. "What was that thing?"

David looked at it and laughed. "That, my friend, is a mayfly. They're harmless."

"They're disgustin'."

"You should see it some seasons." Brad flicked another away. It flitted off, unharmed. "They have to scrape the downtown buildings and the riverfront with snow shovels because they're so thick."

"You know this because …" Rafe prompted.

"I grew up here."

"That's right," Lucas said. "You go to UW-L."

"Hey, Rafe," Justin said, joining them near the bullpen. "Your girl's here."

Rafe stood up and scanned the crowd standing along the fence. He spotted her right away, the early-evening sun glinting off her chestnut hair. His smile threatened to split his face in two as he jogged over to her. He gave her a light peck on the cheek, though he wanted to take her into his arms and kiss her senseless. "Hey, beautiful."

"Hey, yourself," she replied shyly.

He lightly rubbed her arm with his hand. "Is everything all right, Kals?" He used the nickname he'd given her during one of their late-night phone calls.

Confusion flitted through her eyes, then she shook her head. "I'm fine. Great job in Mad-Town."

"Thanks." He kissed her lips. "It would've been better if you'd been there."

She blushed, but stood her ground. "It was for the best. For both of us."

"Will you go out with me after tonight's game?" He grinned. "I have a hankerin' for chocolate chip pancakes."

She giggled, the sound music to his ears. "I think that can be arranged."

Desire flooded him. "I missed that."

"What?"

"Your laugh." He sighed as one of the coaches barked at him from the far left-field corner where the rest of the team was still warming up. "I have to go. Wish me luck?"

She smiled, which sent a whirl of desire through him. "Of course. Good luck, Rafe."

He cupped her cheek and drew her to him for one more kiss. "Thanks, darlin'." He jogged back to the outfield for the pregame huddle.

Kallie still couldn't believe the hottest guy on the baseball team was interested in her. The late-night phone calls when his schedule allowed quickly became addicting. The way he called her "Kals" made her feel like she was the most special person in the world. His Texan drawl really got to her, and she loved hearing his voice. She loved running her fingers through his soft, dark hair, and the way her body molded to his when he held her close. She loved him, period.

She was afraid to tell him.

Kallie thought about their relationship during the All-Star break, and came to the realization that she would always be the one going to him. Whether it was his games or during the off-season, his schedule would always be too hectic for him to come to her. As for her dreams, she wanted to finish her Clinical Laboratory Science degree. Since her uncle passed away from non-Hodgkin's Lymphoma three years ago, she wanted to help with research on finding cures for chronic diseases and cancers.

Kallie wasn't breaking up with him because she wanted to see where they were heading, but they were both young and had their whole lives ahead of them. Rafe had a long, promising career in baseball. He was good enough to make it to the top, and she wanted him to get there.

Kallie stayed for the game because she wanted to see Rafe killing it on the field. He filled out his uniform quite well, and she couldn't keep her eyes off of him. His body was lean, showing promise of developing into an athlete in his prime. He was sexy as sin.

She smiled to herself. They had a date after the game.

In past seasons, if the team had won the first-half pennant they faltered in the second. Not this year. With two weeks left, the Loggers still had the best record in the league. Rafe was strong at short-stop. David had developed into an ace starting pitcher, and Lucas and Harrison were phenomenal in the outfield. The team had an 18-4 record going into the last two weeks.

The whole team had another good game that night, beating Mankato by a score of four to three. Both teams were scoreless through six innings, but David's relief pitcher gave up two runs in the top of the seventh. The Loggers were down three to two going into the bottom of the ninth. Callan hit the ball that would drive in the winning runs.

Kallie felt bad for David, even as she cheered the team victory. Despite his amazing stats, he would end up with a no-decision instead of a win.

After passing his gear to Ed and Sue after of the game, Rafe ushered Kallie to his car and they headed to the restaurant where they'd had their first date. The waitress seated them in the same corner booth and slid menus in front of them. Unlike last time, Rafe sat across from Kallie, instead of next to her. Disappointment slammed into her. Was he putting emotional distance between them as well as physical?

"Same thing as last time, Kals?" he asked.

Nodding, she set the menu aside.

"We're ready to order," he told the waitress before she had a chance to step away.

She raised her eyebrow in surprise, but flipped her pad to a clean page as Rafe ordered a short-stack of chocolate chip pancakes for both of them, along with two tall glasses of milk. The same fare they'd shared the first night.

Kallie smiled at him.

With a nod, the waitress took the menus and headed back to the kitchen.

"Thank you," Kallie said.

Rafe reached across the table and took her hand, caressing her knuckles with his thumb. "My pleasure, darlin'."

The way he called her 'darlin' combined with his thumb skimming her skin made her stomach flip-flop.

"Kallie," he said, capturing her attention. "I've been thinkin'."

Her pulse kicked up tempo at his words, but the waitress chose that moment to drop off their milk. Kallie forced herself to calm down with a deep breath.

"I've been thinkin'," he said again as the waitress stepped away. "I know it's probably not fair to either of us, but I'd like you to come back to Dallas with me in a couple weeks." He rubbed his thumb across the back of her hand. "It'd take care of the problem with your roommates, and I don't think you'd have a problem transferrin' your credits."

Kallie blinked back the sudden rush of tears. His words were everything she'd ever dreamed of, and everything she'd feared. As much as she wanted to go with him – "Rafe, I – I can't," she whispered. "Not because I don't want to."

"Then why –" he started, but she cut him off.

"In a way, it's all happening so fast. I mean, we met two months ago. It isn't fair to either of us. I'd have to pay higher tuition, and I'd have nowhere to live."

"You could stay with me and Mom." Rafe countered.

She refused to acknowledge the idea that he may not be the person with whom she wanted to spend the rest of her life. "If things go the way we want and we both achieve our goals, then we'll have a better chance of making it work." She covered his hand with hers. "We have our whole lives ahead of us. We *both* need this shot, Rafe."

"So, what are you sayin'?" Rafe leaned back. "That we should break up?"

"No." Kallie shook her head. "Only that we don't need to rush into anything. You have an amazing baseball career ahead of you, and I don't want to get in the way of that by making you choose between your dreams and mine." His expression closed, and she could tell she was losing him. Yet, despite her rough spring semester, she solidified her resolve to go into clinical laboratory and cancer research. She owed it to her uncle. Her family.

"But you're telling me I can't have both," he bit out.

"No, Rafe. Please listen." She covered his hand with hers, twining their fingers. "I'm not saying no. I'm saying not right now. You *know* I'm right. If we're meant to be, it'll happen." Kallie took a deep breath and decided to put her cards on the table. "I've never been in love before, Rafe, but I'm pretty sure I'm in love with you. I want you, but I know how much baseball means to you." She looked into his eyes, flinching at the anguish she saw in his green depths. "I'm trying to do the right thing by both of us. I hope you understand. I still want to be the one you share the highs and lows with, like we've been doing all summer."

The waitress brought their food, but suddenly Kallie's appetite fled. Trying to hide it, she buttered her pancakes and drowned them in syrup. Rafe did the same with his. She was about to take the first bite, when he put his hand on hers.

"Kallie."

The way he said her name was both heaven and hell. She met his gaze again.

"You're right," he said at last. "If we're meant to be, it'll happen. But I won't give up on us without a fight." His lips twisted into a wry smile. "Though, if the scouts have their way, I may not finish out in Texas."

One more reason for her to stay in La Crosse. "You mentioned talking with some of them in Madison," she said as her appetite returned.

"I'm determined to give making the minors, and ultimately the majors, my best shot. I've never been in love before, either, but I think I'm fallin' with you." Desire flashed in his eyes, and the corner of his lips kicked up in a sexy half-smile. "If it doesn't work out, I'm comin' back for you."

"You better." Kallie grinned and sipped her milk. "Even if it does, I still want you to come back for me." She finally enjoyed a bite of her pancakes, and he did the same. "Because if you don't, I'm coming after you."

He flashed the boyish grin that always weakened her knees. "So you just want me for the money, is that it?"

Kallie chuckled, her heart lighter than it had been in days. "Of course not," she assured him. "I want to make sure you have a legitimate shot at your dream. I want no less for myself."

Rafe twined their fingers together. "I promise to stay in touch, darlin'."

"And I promise to always answer your call." She took another sip of her milk. "Or call you back if I miss you. While we're in school, I don't see why we can't visit during breaks.

And who knows? Maybe I can go to some of your games in Texas next spring."

Chapter 7

The last weeks of July slid into the lazy summer days of August. Rafe savored the victory during the last regular game of the season. The playoffs started the next day between the four half-season champions; La Crosse and Eau Claire from the North division, and Waterloo and Kenosha from the South. Unless the Loggers were eliminated early, Rafe could play six games in six days.

Rafe had been overjoyed to see that Kallie had made the drive to watch the game in Eau Claire. The Express played at Carson Park, which had seen the likes of greats like Hank Aaron and even Mr. Baseball himself, Bob Uecker. When Rafe walked into the stadium for the second game of the divisional series, he'd felt the baseball history oozing from the front gates.

Back in La Crosse for the Northwoods League championship game, Kallie met Rafe at the fence near the dugout, where they'd met before his first game. He was determined to get her best good-luck kiss ever.

"My beautiful Kals," Rafe greeted her with a smile.

"Hey, handsome," Kallie said.

He cupped her cheek with his palm. "Come to give me my kiss?"

"You know it."

Pleasure spiraled through him when she didn't play coy. He was leaving Monday for Dallas. They had so little time left, and they were past playing silly games. As he leaned over the fence, his lips met hers in the most bittersweet kiss he'd ever felt. His heart thudded as longing rushed through his body, and it frustrated him that she was holding back. He didn't know when he was going to get to kiss her again, and he wanted her to kiss him back with the same amount of passion. "Good luck," she whispered against his lips.

"Thanks, darlin'." He grinned at her again, giving her one last kiss.

Rafe jogged back to his teammates, a high pumping through his system that wasn't entirely due to the adrenaline rush of a big game. Kallie's kisses were a potent narcotic that hooked him fast and hard.

Justin grinned at him when he started stretching for another grueling night between second and third base. "I really think she's your good-luck charm."

Rafe shrugged. "If you believe that sort of thing." A sidelong glance at Justin told Rafe that his teammate wasn't convinced.

Makes two of us.

♥ ♥ ♥

Kallie took her seat next to Amy, though her mind still reeled from her kiss with Rafe. She didn't want to think about him leaving tomorrow. But for tonight, she would savor watching him play one more game. As she and Amy sang the National Anthem with the soloist, energy zinged back and forth through the stands, crackling like electricity. She sat at the edge of her seat as the pregame festivities wrapped up and play began between the Loggers and Kenosha.

David took the mound as the starting pitcher. Despite his vast improvement over the summer, Kenosha still managed to load the bases in the top of the first with two outs. Lucas made an incredible diving catch to retire the side. He slid about four feet through the grass on his chest after snaring the ball with his glove. The crowd – including Kallie – went crazy, chanting Lucas' name as he brushed himself off. He tipped his hat in salute, sending the fans into another frenzied furor.

Rafe took his first at-bat in the bottom of the first, hitting a line drive over the first-baseman's head. The ball landed a scant inch inside the foul line before bouncing into Kenosha's bullpen. By the time the right-fielder came up with the ball, Rafe was sliding into third base.

"Nice triple," Amy remarked, again taking the opportunity to snap shots of the Loggers players' backsides at the plate.

Even though a mere foot separated them on the bench seat, Kallie found it impossible to have a normal conversation without shouting. She nodded in agreement.

Justin stepped up to the plate next, sending his first pitch into shallow left-center. Rafe scored easily from third. Justin barely beat the tag at first base.

Kallie jumped to her feet and yelled at the top of her lungs with elation. Rafe didn't look up at the fans as he disappeared into the dugout.

The bleachers rattled as the fans clapped and stomped to "Bang the Drum All Day," the song that played every time the Loggers scored a run.

She sat back down as Brad took his turn at-bat. Fastball right up the middle. He swung, the crack of the wooden bat echoing off the metal bleachers. The ball sailed into the outfield, climbing higher as it went over the right-fielder's head and out of his reach. The ball finally arced downward on the other side of the fence, hitting the roof of the party cabin before bouncing out of sight.

Pandemonium broke out within the packed stadium. Fans jumped and stomped, clapping along as "Bang the Drum

All Day" erupted through the speakers again. Kallie joined in, swept up with the excitement. Yet she couldn't help thinking that each pitch brought the end of the game closer, and with it her time with Rafe.

"Go Brad!" Amy leapt to her feet and applauded as Brad ran the bases.

They sat back down as Lucas took his second turn in the lineup. An expectant hush descended among the fans. He connected with his second pitch, but grounded out to the shortstop. The next two Loggers batters met similar fates. The crowd cheered as the Loggers started the second inning up three-nothing.

In the top of the third, David struck out the first batter, but walked the second and third.

The field manager called time out and marched out to the mound. Hands on his hips, he talked with David and the catcher. Moments later the catcher walked back to the plate. The field manager spat into the dirt pitcher's mound and returned to the dugout.

The batter connected with the next pitch.

Kallie's heart sank. David looked helpless as he watched the ball sail over the right-field fence Though he managed to strike out the last batter, a dejected hush had settled among the fans.

"I'm gonna get some food," Amy said as the players hustled to the dugout. "Do you want anything while I'm down there?"

"Sure." Kallie handed money to Amy to cover what she wanted. The sea of people at the bottom of the stairs swallowed her friend as she headed toward the concessions.

Two batters later, Kallie wished she had joined her friend. One guy in the row behind and five seats to her right started yelling obscenities at the players and umpires. She wanted to tell him to shut up, but she didn't want to become the target of his ire. La Crosse managed to keep Kenosha from scoring, but was unable to get anything going on offense. The next two innings flew by in short order. Both teams remained strong on defense, and neither was able to score any runs. Rafe made a diving catch, followed by a spectacular dead-on throw to first base that she'd only ever seen in the majors. *Man, he's got a gift!*

The thought further reinforced her decision to not interfere with his baseball future, and eased her nagging conscience for not accepting his offer to transfer her credits.

Amy returned with their food with two outs in the bottom of the fifth inning, her arms laden with a tray piled high with food and two souvenir glasses adorned with a former player who'd made it to the majors.

Kallie took the glass Amy held out as she sat down. "Took you long enough."

"The lines were packed!" Amy lamented. "It took ten minutes just to get out of the food court."

Kallie took her chicken sandwich and onion rings from Amy. "Thanks for remembering the ranch."

"You're welcome." Amy bit into her burger at the same time Callan caught a line drive in mid-air to end the top of the sixth inning.

As Kallie sipped from the straw, she studied the image of the player on the side of the cup. "This will be Rafe one day."

"I believe it," Amy agreed. "That boy's got some mad skills on the field."

The guy behind them was still shouting. The team owner, who was selling peanuts and caramel corn, warned the man to stop or risk getting escorted out of the game. The heckler smarted off to the owner, spewing vulgarities. The owner asked if anyone else in the section wanted peanuts, then turned and went back down to the main walkway. The heckler continued his tirade.

Kallie watched as the owner talked to one of the ushers at the bottom of the stairs.

Not long after, two large security men hustled up the stairs to the top row and forcibly removed the jerk from the stands.

The fans around them applauded and thanked the owner for kicking him out.

"Wow," Amy said after the commotion ended. "That guy was annoying."

"Tell me about it." Kallie finished off her sandwich and set the tray beneath her seat, turning her attention back to the game. "He's been jawing on for the past three innings."

In the top of the seventh David lost zip on his fastball and made the mistake of throwing one up the middle. The Kenosha batter hit a solo home run, much to the dismay of the fans. "Damn!" Amy stomped her foot on the bleacher, making the ice rattle in Kallie's glass.

Kallie giggled as she popped a bite-sized onion ring into her mouth. "Frustrated?"

"Shut up." Amy stuck out her tongue, making Kallie laugh harder. Amy socked her arm.

"Ow!" Kallie rubbed the sore spot, though her friend hadn't put much oomph into the blow.

Lucas ended Kenosha's charge at the top of the inning with a routine fly ball to deep center field.

In the bottom of the seventh, Rafe sent a ball sailing over the infield down the third-base line. It bounced just inside the foul line in front of the Loggers' bullpen, and he was able to get a double out of it. Lucas stepped up to the plate for his turn, hitting the ball into deep center field. It bounced off the wall and dropped to the ground before the outfielder could get to it.

Kallie urged Rafe on as he rounded third and headed for home at the same time the outfielder threw the ball to the second-baseman. Holding her breath, she watched the second-baseman throw to the catcher. Adrenaline pumped through her when the ball sailed wide to the right. The catcher missed Rafe by a mile. With the throwing error, Lucas turned a double into a triple.

She and Amy leapt to their feet and cheered as Rafe trotted back to the dugout, knocking helmets with his teammates after he scored the tying run.

But as much as she enjoyed watching the game, a nervous restlessness stole over her with every pitch. Each half-inning brought her closer to the end of her time with Rafe.

The team stayed sharp the last two innings, shutting down the Kenosha batters one at a time. The relief pitcher gave up two walks and a base hit to load the bases with two outs in the top of the eight, and the field manager brought in the closing pitcher to keep the score tied at five.

The next Kenosha batter connected with the first pitch, sending it toward the right field wall. Lucas made a spectacular catch by jumping above the fence to rob the batter of a grand slam that would've busted the game wide open.

Kallie plugged her ears as the fans roared. Lucas's teammates almost knocked him down as he trotted back into the infield.

"Oh my God!" Amy leapt to her feet. "Did you see that!"

Grinning, Kallie scanned the opposing team's dugout. The players looked shell-shocked. She figured that the robbed grand slam would be the turning point of the game.

The first pitch of the bottom of the ninth inning ratcheted up Kallie's nerves. On the one hand, she didn't want the game to end, because it meant the end of the season and her time with Rafe. On the other, she wanted her home team to win the championship.

The score was still tied when the Loggers took their turn in the ninth. Callan was the first batter in the lineup. He swung at his first pitch, sending it over the first baseman's head and into the corner along the baseline. The outfielder captured it quickly and hurled it toward second base. Callan was already there. Justin stepped into the batter's box next, and waited for his pitch. When he connected, he sent the ball high and deep to left-center field.

Over the fence.

The fans erupted into a deafening roar as Kallie cheered Callan home for the winning run. The rest of the team cleared the dugout and raced after Lucas, who was halfway to the outfield by the time the mob caught up with him and piled on top of him.

"Sheesh," Amy grumbled, grinning. "Don't kill the guy."

Kallie laughed. "I hope no one gets hurt."

Even as dread filled her own heart, Kallie cheered for Rafe and his teammates; they had played their best game of the season and deserved the championship.

He'll be gone tomorrow. The refrain echoed through her head as the team celebrated on the field.

Kallie remained seated, watching them pile on each other with elation. She clapped as the team accepted the trophy, and chuckled when they gave the field manager a Gatorade shower. The fans still in the stands roared with laughter and she snapped photos with her smartphone. Lucas and Rafe accepted the championship banner, then took off running along the warning track as a tribute to the fans that had supported them all season. Amy opted to leave almost right away, claiming she had to work early. After her friend left, Kallie gathered her stuff and moved to the front row behind the third-base dugout, making sure she was easily visible by the time Rafe reached her side of the field. Their gazes met across the distance. He stumbled, eliciting a chuckle from her.

When he got back to his teammates, Rafe passed the banner to Lucas and sprinted back to the dugout gate. He pushed through the throng of people milling about and took the stairs two at a time. Kallie met him at the top. He swung her into his arms. She held tight, inhaling the intoxicating fragrance of hot, sweaty athlete.

"Thank you," he said.

Kallie searched his gaze. "For what?"

"Being here." He kissed her lips. "Come with me."

Before Kallie could respond, Rafe guided her back toward the field with him.

"No, wait!" She pulled at her wrist, but he didn't let go.

Instead, he slid his hand down hers and laced their fingers together as he gathered her in his arms at the base of the stairs. "It wouldn't feel right without you by my side." He kissed her again, his tongue sliding past her lips. "Please. Come with me."

"I can't." She tugged at her wrist again, not wanting to encroach on his time with his teammates. "This is your moment. Share it with the team, not me."

"Kals." He gently cupped her cheek with his hot palm. "You're just as much a part of this team as I am. You've been here with me – for me – every step of the way. I won't do this without you."

The sincerity blazing in his emerald-green eyes zapped her resistance. She placed her hand on his stubbled cheek and nodded. Whooping with delight, he scooped her up and spun her in a circle, then twined their fingers together as they returned to the field.

Justin hugged her. "I hoped Rafe would find you."

Kallie got caught up in a moment she knew she'd never forget. The celebration went on for about an hour. She made sure to stay away from the cameras during the official team photos, though she was pretty sure someone had gotten a few candid shots of her and Rafe together.

"We're going to the restaurant to celebrate," Rafe told her later, naming the place of their first date. "Come with us."

"Rafe, no." Kallie attempted to pull out of his embrace. "You go with your teammates. You guys deserve to celebrate together." Even if it was his last night in La Crosse, she thought glumly. "I can see you tomorrow morning before you leave."

"I don't go home until Monday," Rafe said.

Kallie frowned. "I thought you had to go back tomorrow."

"Nope." He grinned. "I want to spend all day with you."

"That's perfect." She threaded her fingers through his hair. "It's a good thing I'm off tomorrow, too." But as happy as she was to have the extra time with him, she realized saying good-bye to him would be that much harder.

Chapter 8

Kallie pulled the brush back along the High Cliff Park trail in Galesville, revealing the steep but short path to the waterfall at the end of Lake Marinuka.

Rafe gasped. "Oh, wow."

"This is one of my favorite spots." Kallie descended the slippery slope to the rock anchored against the head of the falls.

"I see why you love it." He landed on the boulder after her and wrapped his arms around her waist. "It's so peaceful here."

Balancing precariously against each other, they sat on the boulder, watching as the water carried leaves and twigs lazily over the edge of the dam.

"What do you want to do after graduation?" he asked.

"Get a job in my field, obviously." Kallie leaned into his chest. "I'm still looking for a position involving research for chronic diseases."

His chest rumbled with his chuckle. "That goes without saying."

She sighed. "I can't think that far ahead at this point. But I owe it to my family to go into cancer research."

She'd told him about her uncle during one of their post-game phone calls shortly after the season started.

"I'm sorry about your uncle." He brushed a strand of hair away from her face. "You told me how much he meant to you."

She laid her head on his shoulder. "Thank you."

"Today's been amazin'." He wrapped her tighter. "Have you reconsidered not transferrin' to Dallas?"

Kallie tensed. "No."

"No, you haven't thought about it?" he prodded.

She shook her head. "No, I'm not going."

"But, Kals –"

"No, Rafe. We've been over this." She wanted him to let her go, but the narrow shelf wasn't conducive to a struggle. One false move and they would both end up at the bottom of the twenty-foot drop into Beaver Creek. "I'm not going, so stop asking."

"I want you with me," he argued.

"I know you do," she said, "But just drop it, okay? I want to enjoy this time with you, not spend it fighting."

He kissed her temple. "I don't want to fight either." He sighed and Kallie braced herself for another argument, but to her relief he didn't broach the subject again.

Kallie gazed out over the lake to the west. The water glistened molten gold beneath the late-afternoon sun, the sound of the waterfall lulling her into calmness as Rafe held her close. The crickets and birds serenaded them as time slipped lazily past them.

"As much as I'm enjoying this," Rafe tightened his arms around her, "we should probably get back to La Crosse."

Kallie sighed regretfully. "You're probably right."

Using each other for balance, they each stood on the narrow shelf at the edge of the dam. She ascended the slope first, using nearby trees for leverage and creating footfalls in the soft earth as it crumbled from many years of use. He was close behind her, and soon they were back on the well-worn path that followed the sandstone cliffs. "Do you want to go back to the swinging bridge or through town?"

"As much as I'd enjoy going back to the bridge, we better play it safe and go through town," Rafe said.

"It'll be a bit of a hike back to the car," Kallie warned.

Though he hadn't brought up Dallas again, their argument simmered in the back of her mind.

"Probably no more than going back along the path," he reasoned as they walked to the nearest exit. "I imagine the trail is pretty shaded at this point, making it more treacherous."

Hand-in-hand, they strolled down the sidewalk along the highway. "I learned how to ice skate on Lake Marinuka." Kallie pointed to the building at the corner of Main Street and the highway. "That antiques store there used to be a department store."

"That's a pretty gazebo." He indicated the structure in the Square.

"We got our first puppy there." Kallie grinned. "He would jump into the back of the sled with us as we sailed down the hill. But if we put him in by himself, we chased an empty sled to the bottom."

He chuckled. "Nice."

"Those boarded-up windows used to be a furniture store," she said. "Before that, a hardware store. A friend of my mom's lived in the apartments upstairs for a while."

"What else can you tell me about this town?" He seemed genuinely interested.

Kallie looked around as they walked down Main Street toward the swinging bridge. "That pharmacy used to be a grocery store. The library used to be the police station, and the police station is now where the library used to be." She pointed to a small laundromat tucked between the library and the boarded-up furniture store. "My sister Olivia and I used to race laundry carts there."

His green eyes twinkled in the waning twilight. "My mama would've whupped me if I'd ever done that."

"It was fun." Kallie grinned. "Until Olivia spun me around too fast and I tipped over."

He laughed. "Good God!"

"Good times." They reached the intersection next to the Masonic Lodge. Kallie pointed to a warehouse, which had been converted into artist studios and a small café. "We had hot chocolate there after we finished sledding."

"Where's the hill?"

"The sledding hill?"

She turned and faced up the street toward the police station and post office. "See that arrow at the end of the block? The hill is just beyond that meadow."

He grabbed her hand. "Show me."

Laughing at his enthusiasm, she grabbed his hand and they dodged traffic as they crossed the busy highway. They dashed up the street to the house where she'd spent the first seven years of her life. Kallie could just barely make out the ruts left behind by tires. Her dad and their neighbors had taken turns mowing the field. While it had overrun with weeds, she still picked out a path to the slope. Soft swishing of grasses behind her indicated that Rafe was close by.

He wrapped his arms around her when she drew to a halt at the end of the path.

Melancholy filled her heart as she gazed down her beloved sledding hill. Downed trees had encroached, making the slope too dangerous for recreation. "It wasn't like this back then."

He held her tight. "It happens that way sometimes. Nature has a way of taking back what's hers."

She nodded, unable to speak past the lump in her throat.

"Come on, Kals." He kissed her neck.

They turned around and he gave her a piggyback ride across the field. He almost dropped her twice. The second was partly her fault because neither could stop laughing. She climbed down when they reached the street, and they strolled back to her truck, hand-in-hand at a more leisurely pace.

Minutes later Kallie turned onto the highway heading back to La Crosse.

"Do you like ice cream?" she asked as they entered the freeway near Holmen.

He laughed. "Love it."

"Good." Five minutes later she took the freeway exit toward Minnesota, then jumped onto the interstate. "The

Sweet Shop has fantastic ice cream and homemade chocolates."

Ten minutes later Kallie parked her truck on Caledonia Street in front of one of La Crosse's oldest businesses. The neon lights illuminated the storefront, and a little bell dinged when she opened the door.

Kallie led him to the counter where they could peruse the list of flavors tacked to the back wall. They placed their orders for root beer floats. She tried paying, but Rafe insisted that he get it. He gave the young woman behind the counter a bill, telling her to keep the change. Afterwards, he guided her to the booths in the back of the store. The blue wooden booths were too small for them to sit side-by-side, so he slid in across from her.

A few minutes later the shop worker dropped off their desserts and they both dug in.

The combination of root beer and vanilla ice cream always reminded her of when she was a kid. Her dad gave both her and Livvie the treats when they got home from school. The sound of air sucking through a straw made her grin. Rafe had finished his, though her glass was still half-full.

A straw encroached on her drink.

"Hey!" Chuckling, she snatched her mug out of his reach. "Leave mine alone!"

"Come on," he teased. "You can share."

Sticky root beer and ice cream dripped onto her hand as he reached again for her glass.

"Please?" He gave her a pleading look that should've been childish, but on him was adorable.

"You shouldn't have finished yours so fast." Bringing her straw to her lips, she enjoyed teasing him as she finished her float.

"I couldn't help it." He belched loudly, quickly excusing himself. "Man, that was good."

Kallie giggled. "See what happens when you drink too fast?"

"I'll keep that in mind for next time." He grinned.

She glanced at the clock as the waitress cleared the frosted glass mugs. "There's one more thing I want to share with you."

Rafe gave her a puzzled frown. "I can't imagine what that would be. Today's been absolutely perfect."

"Call it coming full circle, if you like." Kallie started her truck and doubled back to George Street. Zipping through traffic, she noted the rapidly-disappearing sun in the western sky, hoping she had enough time to make it.

"Hey, Indy racer." The laughter in his voice didn't fully mask his concern. "Slow down."

Kallie eased up on the accelerator, dropping her speed to exactly four miles over the posted limit signs as she followed the streets toward the eastern bluffs. "I hope we have enough time to make it." A couple minutes later she turned left onto Main Street and headed for Bliss Road.

She dropped her speed and followed the curving esses that climbed the steep grade up the hill. She finally came to the turn that would take them to the overlook. The eastern sky had darkened, but on the other side the sun's brilliant rays still illuminated the Mississippi River Valley. Ten minutes later Kallie parked her truck in the lot and turned off the motor. Rafe put his hand on her arm.

"Kallie, wait." He drew her to him, cupping her face in his hands. "I'll never forget today, or the time we've shared." He kissed her as she rested her hands on his chest.

His heart pounded beneath her palms. Her eyes drifted shut as his mouth moved over hers, hard to soft, curve to angle. His tongue glided along the seam of her lips and she opened in invitation. By mutual agreement they deepened the kiss, a low moan rumbling his flesh and into her fingertips.

A response echoed through her, making her wish they were both at a time in their lives when they were ready to make a commitment. Because the inevitable conclusion wasn't something either of them was prepared for, Rafe broke away first.

Kallie's lashes fluttered as she blinked open her eyes, locking her gaze onto his as her heart threatened to burst from her chest.

"Let's watch the sunset together?" she asked.

He gave her a lopsided grin and nodded.

They exited the truck and strolled hand-in-hand to the vantage point overlooking the city, Kallie pointing out the various landmarks she recognized around the city and beyond. She even showed him the headlands of Iowa in the far southern distance.

A small crowd gathered at the top of Granddad Bluff, which was normal. She ignored the people milling about, content to focus solely on Rafe. At last, she strode to the fence, leaning her arms against the top rail. Rafe stood behind her, wrapping his arms around her waist. She leaned her head against his chest, neither of them saying anything as they watched the orange ball of flame slowly sink towards the cliffs of Minnesota.

Fingers of pink and yellow fanned into the blues and indigos of night, the stars appearing overhead as the sun finally disappeared over the western horizon. Crickets and birds chirped as dusk fell.

He kissed the side of her neck. "Thank you."

"For what?" Her voice caught, the words coming out on a croak.

"I wasn't sure how much more perfect this day could get, but you've proved me wrong." He turned her around to face him, caressing her arms with his hands. "Finishin' out this amazin' day with you at the spot where we first bumped into each other was the best." He brushed his lips lightly over hers. "I love you, Kallie."

Again, their disagreement popped into her head. *I can't go with him,* she reminded herself with a conviction she didn't feel. *There's too much at stake. I can't risk it.*

Tears stung her eyes as their gazes locked again. His reflected the starlight and possibilities of the future. "I love you, too, Rafe."

Chapter 9

Kallie wasn't sure how she made it through the first half of the fall semester. She'd bumped into Brad a few times between classes, and he'd taken the time to chat with her.

"He still asks about you," Brad said on one of their walks around campus around Halloween.

"I know," Kallie had replied. "He still calls me, too."

"Don't give up on him," he'd advised. "Rafe's one of the good ones."

"I won't," she'd promised, though each day apart was making it harder for her to remember his touch.

She walked to class the Friday before Thanksgiving, the crisp autumn air carrying the promise of winter's chill. Her phone jingled with Rafe's special ringtone. Smiling, she answered the call.

"Hey, beautiful."

Her smile threatened to split her face. "Hey, yourself."

"I'm in between classes and only have a few minutes, but I wanted to hear your voice." He sighed. "What are your plans for next weekend?"

"I'll probably spend it studying." She'd fallen behind in one of her phlebotomy classes. "I can't seem to wrap my head around the pathology stuff."

"Better you than me," he teased.

"Shut up." She stuck out her tongue at his chuckle, though she knew he couldn't see it. "Do you know how many blood-borne diseases there are in this world?"

"Probably more than I want to know."

She giggled. "You're probably right."

"You're a smart woman, Kals. You'll figure it out." The line went silent for a couple of moments. "The reason I called was to ask about your Thanksgiving plans. Would you be willin' to come here?" He asked the question hesitantly.

"Oh … I –" Stunned, Kallie wasn't sure how to respond. "I'd love to, but –" She broke off. "I'd have to talk to my parents first." She'd need their help to pay for the ticket.

He asked more strongly. "If they're okay with it, will you come?"

"I do want to see you again…" she trailed off, unsure how they'd be able to afford the flight. She'd cut back her hours at the grooming salon so she'd have more time to study. The downside of working less meant there was less money after her tuition and fees were paid.

"But…" he prompted.

"I can't really afford it," she finally admitted, thinking of her dwindling finances. If things kept spiraling downward, she'd have to take out a student loan to pay for her senior year.

"We'll work something out," he assured her. "I promise."

"You need to stay home and study," Kallie's mom said from her seat at the head of the family kitchen table later that evening.

"Honey, it wouldn't hurt for her to go," Dad rallied from the seat at her left. "She's been mooning around the house for the last four months"

"And not focusing on school," Mom pointed out. "She's at risk of getting put on academic probation."

"I'm sorry." Kallie sat opposite her father. "I know I'm struggling. But it's not from mooning over Rafe. My phlebotomy class is kicking my butt."

"Why do you think you deserve this break?" Mom asked. Not in a mean tone, but one that said 'here's your chance to convince me otherwise. Make it count.'

Kallie stared into the steaming mug of cocoa in front of her, taking a moment to compose her thoughts. "I don't disagree that my grades aren't where I want them to be," she started, "but I've been studying really hard this semester, and I think a break will help with the burnout I'm starting to deal with." She sipped her cocoa, the melted marshmallows creating a gooey barrier between her lips and the liquid, and then gave her mom an imploring look. "I miss him, Mom. I really want to see him again."

With sympathy in his deep blue eyes, Dad reached across the table and placed his hand on hers. "I know you do, punkin." He turned to his wife. "What do you say, Mama? Should we let her go?"

"I don't know." Mom leaned back in her chair. "I think maybe you're trying to take on too much. I'm still concerned about your grades. And what about your job? Are you able to get off work at such short notice?"

"I'll talk to my boss." Kallie was confident her appointments wouldn't be a problem. "What can't be rearranged, we'll reschedule."

Mom regarded her with steady observation. "If you can rearrange your appointments, and if you get better scores on your mid-terms this week, we'll help you pay for your ticket."

Kallie leapt out of her chair, jostling the table with so much force that it sent the cocoa in her mostly-full cup sloshing over the side, and wrapped her arms around her mother's neck. "Thank you, Mom!"

"I expect you to hold up your end of the bargain," Mom said. "This isn't a freebie."

Mom's words diminished some of Kallie's exuberance, but she gave her parents a grateful smile as she sat back down.

"Finish your cocoa," Mom said. "I'll look into travel arrangements for you."

Her eyelids drooping, Kallie took a sip of water from the travel bottle as she joined the exodus down the jet way on Wednesday afternoon. *Who in their right mind ever willingly gets up so freaking early?* Even with morning classes, she didn't have to get up until six-thirty.

Between Rafe, Kallie and her parents, the only flight they'd been able to afford was the six-thirty morning departure from La Crosse. She'd ruffled a few feathers with her coworkers, but her supervisor helped rearrange her appointments to have the next five days off. But when she got back next week, she'd have to cover shifts for each of the groomers.

Her alarm clock went off at four-thirty so she had enough time to go through the security checkpoint. Thankfully her layover in Minneapolis had only been an hour, and she spent most of the flight to Dallas asleep.

Though her dad had encouraged her to go, Mom had wanted her to stay home and study as she was on the cusp of letting another class get away from her. Kallie decided to make the trip and give herself a chance to refresh. She hoped it would help her retain more information when she hit the books again.

Too tired to descend the stairs, she rode the escalator to the basement of the Dallas-Fort Worth terminal and followed the signs to the baggage carousels.

When she entered the area, Rafe stood next to her carousel, holding a sign with her name on it. He was even more handsome than she'd remembered. Her knees almost buckled on the escalator, but she still managed to run into his arms.

He swept her up, kissing her fiercely. "I've missed you, Kals," he said against her lips. "Thank you for comin'." He kissed her again, then led her out of the terminal.

Kallie faltered a step when she saw the beautiful older woman standing next to his car, the breeze filtering through her long, black hair.

He tightened his arm around Kallie's waist, propelling her forward. "My mom, Florinda," he said by way of explanation. "She couldn't wait to meet you."

"You may call me Ms. Donaldson." Rafe's mother extended her hand. "So, you're the woman who's captured my son's heart."

Kallie's smile faltered as she accepted the greeting. Even Rafe looked a little stunned at his mother's stiff formality. "He's got mine, too."

"I'm glad to hear that." Ms. Donaldson broke contact first. As they climbed into the car, his mom insisted Kallie sit up front with her, relegating Rafe to the back seat. "So, Kallie," she said her gaze shrewd and assessing as she started the motor, "tell me about yourself."

I see where he got his eyes. Hesitantly, Kallie gave an overview of her life back in Wisconsin, still taken slightly aback by the lack of welcome from Rafe's mom. She didn't mind that some of the questions were pointed as Ms. Donaldson asked about college and Kallie's plans for the future, and the other woman seemed pleased that Kallie had goals of her own.

Yet Kallie still sensed standoffishness in the older woman's demeanor.

Thirty minutes later they turned into the driveway of a charming two-story bungalow on a quiet tree-lined lane. Bright purple petunias, pink dianthus and purple and yellow pansies marched up both sides of the walkway, while a red oak tree towered above the two-story house. As she neared, Kallie spotted a wicker swing hanging from the rafters on the porch. She pictured curling up with Rafe on the plump cushions covered in bright spring flowers, talking as they rocked back and forth while the sun sank into the horizon. She smiled at the image.

Ms. Donaldson exited the car and strode to the front door without so much as a backward glance.

Puzzled, Kallie opened her door and slid her feet to the ground. "Did I do something wrong?" she asked Rafe.

"It's fine," he said. "Mom's just got a lot on her mind. She's still working two jobs, and has had a tough go if it these past couple of months."

"But if she didn't want me here –"

"She does," he quickly assured her. "She told me she was anxious to meet you."

He lifted her luggage from the trunk and led her up the path to the house. The sight made her think of him waiting on her hand-and-foot, and she giggled as they climbed the steps to the deep front porch.

Stopping at the threshold, Kallie took a deep breath and adjusted her grip on the duffel. Something inside told her that she and Rafe were taking a huge step forward in their relationship with her being there. Quelling the queasiness churning in her gut, she entered the house.

A quick glance around gave her the impression of a light, airy house that was very much a home, at odds with the less-than-warm greeting from Rafe's mom.

"Thank you, Ms. Donaldson." The front door opened up into the living room, inviting one to plop onto the overstuffed sofa and kick back after a hard day's work. Abstract paintings and portraits lined the walls and religious knickknacks adorned most of the available shelf space. The alcove space above the rocking chair was a shrine to the Virgin Mary. Kallie fought the urge to wrinkle her nose. She attended services at a Lutheran church back home, but the number of figurines was overwhelming even for her. "I love your home."

"Thank you." Rafe's mom took the suitcase from Rafe as he entered behind them. A tour of the first floor proved that Kallie's impression from the living room was accurate. The kitchen, while tiny, utilized every inch of space. A rack hung from the ceiling, copper pots and pans dangling from hooks. A round pine table sat in one corner while the appliances flanked the other two walls.

Kallie noted the lack of dishwasher, and a quick peek into the utility room off the back of the kitchen showed only a washing machine. No dryer.

The missing appliances reminded her of what Rafe said when he'd been in La Crosse, that he and his mom had had a difficult life, and she'd taken some of the luxuries her parents could afford for granted.

The faint aroma of baking cornbread followed them as they left the kitchen.

Finished with the lower level, they climbed the stairs to the second. There were three bedrooms. Florinda had the big one at the end of the hall, and Rafe's was at the other end. They were separated by a smaller guest bedroom and the second-floor bathroom.

"Unfortunately, you and Rafe will have to share the bathroom," Ms. Donaldson said with displeasure.

"I'm sure it'll be fine," Kallie replied. Suddenly an image flashed before her eyes, of the two of them side-by-side in front of the mirror, him shaving in nothing but a towel while she brushed her teeth in her pajamas. She stumbled, catching the toe of her sneaker on the top step. Rafe was there, his hand on her back.

"Careful," he said in a low voice.

When she turned, she saw laughter glinting in his dark-green eyes. With a quick dart of her tongue out the left corner of her lips, she made for the bedroom that would be hers for the weekend. Her back was to him so she didn't catch his reaction, but his low chuckle reached her ears.

Like the rest of the house, the room was light and airy. Draped over the plain double bed was a lavender floral bedspread. Egg-shell-colored paint covered the walls, the medium-pile carpet a soft cream. The dresser tucked in the corner appeared to be mass-produced pressed wood, but it was still functional. Kallie set her duffel on the floor at the foot of the bed. "Thank you, Ms. Donaldson."

"Dinner's at six. Freshen up, and we'll see you then." Her footsteps echoed down the hall.

Kallie sat on the bed, exhaustion sweeping over her.

Rafe set her suitcase next to the duffel. "Ready to run screaming yet?"

"No." She smiled, her fatigue melting away. "Though I was expecting a warmer welcome."

"That puzzled me too. I'd gotten the impression she'd been lookin' forward to meetin' you." Rafe sat next to her on the bed, though he left the door open for propriety. "She can be overwhelmin' at times, but she's my mom."

"If you get the chance to meet my family, you better prepare for the Spanish Inquisition." Her parents' work schedules hadn't permitted them to attend any of his games, and Livvie wasn't into sports. "I'm sorry you didn't get to meet them when you were in La Crosse."

"So am I." He stood up and pulled her to her feet, wrapping his arms around her. "I'm glad you're here. I missed you."

She buried her nose in his neck and inhaled deeply, the clean scent of his aftershave intoxicating her. "I've missed you, too."

"We better get downstairs before Mom starts throwin' ice cubes at us." He grinned wryly, letting her go. "Her way of keepin' us from gettin' too cozy."

Kallie giggled. "Is she afraid I have designs on her son's virtue?"

"Maybe she thinks I have designs on yours."

Desire flooded through her. "I wouldn't mind if you did."

His grin turned wolfish. "I'm glad. But not here, I'm afraid." He sobered. "We better get out of here. Mom really will chuck ice at us."

She laughed again as he escorted her to the first floor. Wonderful aromas permeated the air, and she found herself drifting toward the kitchen. When she entered, Ms. Donaldson stirred a stew of some sort on the stove, and the aroma of baking bread was stronger.

The odor of peppers hit Kallie hard, making her stomach roil. She turned and pushed past Rafe, heading for the front door. When she got outside, she made a beeline for the porch swing. Sitting down, she gulped in huge lungfuls of air in an attempt to dispel the nausea.

Rafe joined her a few moments later, concern knitting his brow. "Hey, are you okay?"

Closing her eyes, she rested her head against his shoulder. Was it her imagination, or did he feel more muscular than he had back in August? "I am now. Thanks."

"What happened?"

The worry in his voice touched her heart. "I'm sorry. I should've told you I'm allergic to peppers." Kallie gulped in another breath. "I had to get out of there before I got sick. I – I hope I didn't offend your mom."

"I'm sure it'll be fine," he said.

"Is everything all right?" Ms. Donaldson joined them on the porch, her voice conveying her concern.

"Fine, Mom," Rafe said. "But Kallie's allergic to peppers."

"I'm sorry, sweetie." Ms. Donaldson's voice filled with compassion for the first time since Kallie's arrival. "I'll make something else for you. How does a turkey and spinach omelet sound?"

Kallie raised her head and nodded. "Thank you."

Rafe followed his mom into the kitchen to help finish dinner.

"Why didn't you tell me?" she asked as he grabbed the eggs and butter from the fridge.

"I'm sorry, Mom." He set the items on the counter and reached for the turkey. "She just told me on the porch."

"What's done is done." She brushed past him and grabbed the cheese and a container of spinach. "I won't have the poor girl starve while she's here."

"Are you really okay with making somethin' different for her?" he asked.

She leveled a stern glare at him, and Rafe recoiled slightly. Kallie may not have offended his mother, but he sure had.

"Rafe Edward Donaldson, if I was put out by it, I wouldn't be doin' it."

"What about tomorrow?" He added sliced mushrooms to the ingredients. "Do you need help with anythin'?"

"It won't be a problem. I only have a couple dishes with peppers in them." She cracked eggs into a bowl and whisked them with a fork, adding a small amount of water to the mix. "I have all the cookin' handled for tomorrow. You two can set the table beforehand." Mom dropped a pat of butter into the heated skillet.

Despite her words and calm demeanor, Rafe had a feeling his mom wasn't too pleased that he'd brought his girlfriend home. "Mom, are you really okay with Kallie bein' here?"

"She wouldn't be here if I wasn't." Her back was to him as she swished the butter around the pan and dumped in the eggs.

"It's just –" He shook his head, not wanting to sound ungrateful. He let the subject drop for the time being. "Thank you."

"Dinner will be ready soon. Get that girl of yours and go wash."

"Yes, ma'am." Rafe smiled and dashed back to the porch, anxious to be at his girlfriend's side. *His girlfriend.* He liked the sound of that.

"Is your mom mad?" Kallie asked when he sat next to her again.

"No." He shook his head. At least, he didn't think she was. "She just asked why I didn't tell her sooner."

"I'm sorry. I didn't think to tell you." She rested her head on his shoulder again. "My mom's allergic too, so we don't usually have a problem at home.

He wrapped her in his arms, the feel of her beneath his touch detonating intense desire inside him. He wanted to hold her forever. "Mom said dinner's almost ready."

Rafe sighed regretfully as they both stood. His arm around her waist, he guided her across the porch to the front door. A shrill wolf-whistle from the sidewalk stopped him in his tracks. He turned, and saw a guy he knew from high school. "Hey, George."

"Hey, Rafe." George catcalled again. "Who's the babe?"

Kallie tensed behind Rafe, and he tightened his hold around her waist. "She's my girlfriend." His tone told George to back off. He and George had been friends in high school, but George had taken Talia to Prom even though he knew she and Rafe had been dating. Talia's excuse for accepting was that she felt Rafe hadn't been giving her the attention she'd felt she'd deserved. Not only had it caused a rift between him and Talia, but also between him and George. Seeing George again, Rafe realized that rift hadn't fully healed. "Mom's calling us for dinner. I'll talk to you later."

"Wait." George called back. "Some of us are gonna get a game going on Friday. Wanna come?"

Rafe sighed. "Yeah. Sure. Call me later." He turned to Kallie. "We better get inside before Mom starts complainin' about cold food."

Kallie giggled. He loved hearing her laugh, the sound twisting his insides in a good way as he followed her back into the house.

He refused to get drawn into another fight with his former classmate.

Chapter 10

Kallie sat in the bleachers of the baseball diamond on Friday afternoon, watching with the other ladies as Rafe played sandlot baseball with some boys he'd grown up with. Even though they were all over twenty-one, a few of them still cracked immature jokes like they were in high school. One of them made a crude sexual remark to George. George laughed, but Rafe just glowered at them both.

She could tell Rafe's difficult childhood had left its mark on him. He wasn't as carefree and relaxed as his friends. His expression was fierce. He played like he was in game seven of the World Series and his team was down three runs in the eighth inning.

From some of the comments Kallie had caught from the other women, she gathered that Rafe had only had one other serious girlfriend in his past. It seemed their friends were still hoping Rafe would take her back.

Her heart skipped a beat.

The ping from the aluminum bat caught her attention. She looked up, watching as the ball sailed over the outfield wall. Leaping to her feet, Kallie cheered Rafe on as he ran the bases.

"So, Kallie," one of the girls said, "where are you from?"

Kallie turned to the attractive blonde sitting behind her. The woman could've been a model; her features were irritatingly perfect and not a strand of white-blonde hair was out of place. "Wisconsin."

"Talia's gonna be pissed."

The words were whispered, but Kallie heard them anyway. Turning to the woman who reminded her of Esther Dean from Pitch Perfect, she asked, "Who's Talia?"

The girls shuffled in their seats, refusing to meet her eyes. The blonde finally said, "She's the one who's been saving herself for Rafe since Kindergarten. You're gonna have to wrestle him away from her."

"Honey, you better bring your A game," said the curvy girl with mahogany skin and smooth, dark hair. "You're gonna have a fight on your hands."

Kallie didn't let them see her flinch as she turned back to the playing field. She knew giving him her heart wasn't enough. Ultimately, he would have to choose her, as well, in order for their relationship to work. *What if he doesn't choose me?*

Kallie caught whispers of snide comments from the two women who were apparently still loyal to Talia, but for the most part the others were more cordial, if less than welcoming. Kallie did her best to shrug off the passive-aggressive comments from the blonde and her dark-haired friend, but she had a feeling it was going to be a long afternoon.

After the game Kallie and Rafe followed George and the rest of the players to the local pizza place. She'd had her reservations, mainly because of George. He'd apologized for his behavior before the game – though she got the impression he was apologizing for more than that – and he'd turned out to be a halfway decent guy. But she still wasn't sure about the other players' girlfriends.

When Kallie and Rafe climbed into his car after the game, neither spoke. The silence stretched until she thought she'd scream. "Who's Talia?" She didn't want to sound desperate, but needed reassurance from Rafe that the other woman was in his past. Jealousy was a new emotion for her, and she didn't like it.

Rafe grimaced. "I figured she'd be mentioned sooner or later." He sighed. "We were high school sweethearts. It wasn't serious for me, so I ended it when I decided to make a career playing baseball."

"But it was for her."

"I don't know. I guess, maybe." He shrugged while braking for a red light. "I wasn't ready for that kind of relationship so I broke it off."

"Did she know it wasn't serious?"

He flexed his fingers on the wheel, his only outward sign of nerves. "I told her it wasn't." He leveled a direct look at Kallie. "Whether she accepted it or not is on her. I wasn't interested in datin' after high school because of baseball. Regardless, she's in the past." The light changed green and he pressed the accelerator, returning his attention back to the road. "I got a full baseball scholarship for college, and didn't want to jeopardize it by not giving my all."

Kallie bit her lip. "Am I –" she broke off, not sure if she wanted the answer to her question.

He reached over and grasped her hand in his. "Are you … what?"

She should have realized he wouldn't let it go. "Am I jeopardizing those chances now?" She ended the question on a whisper. "What if this isn't the right time for us?"

He kept his attention on the road, but the muscle ticking in his jaw meant that he'd heard her.

Ten minutes later, Rafe pulled into the pizzeria parking lot and cut the motor. He turned in his seat, cupping her cheek in his warm, calloused palm. "I don't have all the answers,

Kallie. Will I make it to the majors? Will I even get drafted? What if I'm not good enough to play pro ball? All of those questions haunt me almost every second of every day. But one thing I do know is that my life would be empty without you. Last summer you showed me that, with the right person by my side, I can have baseball and love." He took a deep breath and let it out slowly. "Being with you these last couple of days has only solidified what we have."

She gasped as his lips claimed hers. The raw power of their kiss set her blood on fire.

Rafe rested his forehead against hers, his breath heavy against her cheek. "We better go inside."

Kallie blinked, confused. "What?"

He threaded his fingers through her hair, his gaze intense. "Kallie, let's get inside before I take you someplace where we can be alone."

Their relationship was still new, and despite his assurances so far, there were still too many uncertainties about their future. She feared having sex would spoil it for both of them. Butterflies danced in her stomach. "We better not."

His chuckle rumbled through his solid chest. She felt it beneath her hand as he kissed her again. They got out of the car and walked into the restaurant, hand-in-hand. Aromas of oregano, garlic and spicy pepperoni greeted her as they entered the pizza parlor. The tables were covered with red-and-white checkered table cloths. Chianti bottles wrapped in raffia served as holders for red and white taper candles flickering gently from the slow-moving fans.

The rest of Rafe's friends were already there, along with the same women from the bleachers. Her steps faltered, but Rafe squeezed her hand

"It's okay," he whispered. "I'm with you."

Despite her earlier misgivings, Kallie enjoyed the rest of the afternoon at the pizzeria. Rafe's friends were good people, and, though not all of them opened their arms to her, they did treat her with kindness. The Esther Dean-lookalike kept glaring daggers at her but she shrugged it off, chalking it up to the other woman's loyalty to Talia.

They left the restaurant about an hour later. Kallie mentioned the woman's behavior as if it didn't bother her, but some of the barbs had stung. Rafe explained the friendship between her and Talia, confirming what Kallie had already deduced from their brief encounter.

After a quiet dinner with Ms. Donaldson, Kallie and Rafe drove back to the ball field. He parked in a cleared area and opened the sunroof.

"I wish you didn't have to go back." He sighed, twining her fingers with his. "This weekend has been the best."

Kallie leaned against the headrest, closing her eyes. "I know." She looked at him. He was so cute it hurt. "We have six months left until graduation." She flashed a cheeky grin. "We've gotten this far. Surely six months won't kill us."

He chuckled. "No, it won't." He paused. "But what if I make it to the minors?"

"Then you're halfway to your dream." Kallie turned to face him. "Rafe, it isn't like we'll never see each other again."

"I hope not. Seein' you, holdin' you again, has given me peace of mind. I firmly believe we're on the right path, and there's no one I can think of that I want to spend the rest of my life with than you, Kallie." He cupped her cheek, stroking his thumb along her lower lip. "I love you."

"I love you, too, Rafe." She turned her head and pressed her lips to his hot, callused palm. "I believe in our love, and I know we'll be together again."

"Try to keep me away," he said with a mock growl.

They kissed. Long, slow, and sweeter.

She wrapped her arms around his neck, storing up as many memories as she could, so she'd have something to get her through until she could see him again.

Chapter 11

"What do you want to do today?" Rafe asked Saturday after breakfast. They were curled up on the sofa in his living room.

Kallie shrugged. "What do you normally do on the weekends?"

"You'd laugh if I told you." His face heated as she put her hand on his arm.

"No, I won't."

"Okay." He took a deep breath. *Here goes.* "I do my homework on Saturday mornings."

"Well, better than Sunday nights."

Her tone was light, but he heard the smirk. He pretended to be hurt. "I thought you said you weren't gonna laugh."

"I'm not."

He crossed his arms. "Sure sounds like it."

Kallie rested her hand on his chest, and he was certain he'd never get tired of her touch. She caught him by surprise when she kissed the tip of his nose affectionately.

"You're so cute when you pout."

He couldn't stop the chuckle that rumbled through him. "Cute, huh?"

She grinned playfully. "Yeah. Cute."

"I'll show you 'cute.'" Capturing her in his arms, Rafe tickled her sides.

She squealed, trying to escape. But he was faster, and stronger. He pinned her against the sofa with one arm and tickled her with the other.

"Rafe! Stop!" she gasped between giggles.

"Take it back," he mock-threatened.

"Rafe!" She gripped his arm, but didn't try fighting him off.

"Take it back," he teased.

She squirmed against his grasp as he tickled her side. Tears streamed down her cheeks from laughing. He thought she'd never looked more beautiful. His hand traveled up her torso, connecting with the soft flesh at the side of her breast. The contact was accidental, but it set something off inside him. As much as he wanted to let his baser instincts kick in, he suppressed his desire as he tickled her.

"Stop!" she shrieked, wriggling to escape his hold. "Okay! I – I take –"

"Rafe, quit torturing the poor girl."

His mother's voice cut through the commotion. He immediately sat up, bringing her with him as he held her close, rubbing his hand over her arm and shoulder. "Sorry, Mom."

"You should be," she admonished. "I could hear her screaming in the backyard."

Kallie blushed, her damp face blossoming with color. Mom brushed Rafe aside and steered her away from him. Kallie was still trying to catch her breath.

"Come with me, dear. Let's get you something to drink."

Stunned, Rafe could only stare as his mom guided his girlfriend into the sun-drenched kitchen. It was the first time she hadn't been distant with Kallie. Was she finally accepting that it was serious between them? He shook his head and followed in their wake. He watched as his mom handed Kallie a tissue and set a glass of water in front of her.

"What was that all about?" Mom asked.

Rafe cringed as he hovered outside the door. He knew that tone. It usually meant he was in trouble.

"It was stupid, really." Kallie sipped from her glass. "I called him cute, and the next thing I knew, he'd pinned me down, tickling me."

Rafe stilled, mixed emotions churning in him. And he fell in love with her even more. She'd told the truth without sugarcoating. She was honest, and had a high level of integrity.

I'm doomed.

"My son is pretty cute."

Heat burned his face. *Aw, Mom!*

"I really like your son, Ms. Donaldson."

Uh-oh. Rafe continued watching, still partially hidden in the doorway.

"I'm glad, dear. He really likes you, too." His mom put her hand on Kallie's shoulder. "Having met you, I'm happy to say the same. And please, call me Flor."

Pleasure rushed through Rafe. Mom only allowed her close circle of friends to call her by the nickname.

"Thank you, Flor." Kallie ran her thumb over her glass, wiping away condensation. "The truth is ..." she paused. His heart sank a little. "...I'm in love with Rafe."

His mom didn't speak, but she tensed up.

"That's why this is so hard," Kallie continued. "I know he loves me, too."

"Kallie –"

Kallie held up her hand, cutting off his mom. "Please let me finish. Rafe and I have talked about it, and we both agreed to graduate school first. And I won't stand in the way of his baseball career."

Rafe's heart pounded. Mom gaped at his girlfriend. She then closed her mouth, wrapping her hands around her own glass. He could see the gleam of approval shining in her eyes from his hiding spot by the door.

A ghost of a smile flickered on Mom's lips. "You can come in now."

It took Rafe a moment to realize she was talking to him. Heat flooded his cheeks and he grimaced. He entered the kitchen and sat in the chair next to Kallie's, twining their fingers on the table. He braced himself for a lecture.

Mom surprised him when she patted his arm and smiled. "You have a good woman, Rafe."

He smiled back. "I know."

"Go," she said. "Spend the rest of the day with her. I'll hold dinner until you get back."

Kallie slid into Rafe's car, his hand on her wrist. Closing her door, he slid behind the wheel.

"What would you like to do?" he asked, buckling his seatbelt.

"Uh-uh." Kallie shook her head, laughing. "I'm still recovering from the last time you asked me that."

Rafe grinned as he started the ignition. "I promise my hands won't leave the wheel."

"I'm gonna hold you to that," she said. *Payback time.* "What do you normally do after you finish your homework?"

She put her hand on his lower thigh, tapping her fingertips in time to the classic country song pouring through the speakers. She fought her grin when he gasped. "Problems?" She smirked when he grimaced. "Well? I'm waiting."

"I either hit the weight room or –" his breath hissed through his teeth when her hand slid higher "– or I hit the –" another gasp "– batting cages."

She drew her index finger down the inside of his leg back to the knee, lightly scraping her nail along the inseam. He jumped, his foot lightly slipping off the gas. His hand reached for hers, but she put it back on the steering wheel.

"You promised." She giggled at his pained expression.

"You're mean."

She grinned. "Payback's a witch. That's for tickling me earlier."

He chuckled. "Okay, I deserved that." He shifted in his seat, turning his attention back to the road. "Do you want to see a movie or something?"

The possibility of cuddling with him in a dark theater held appeal, but it would more than likely lead to something they weren't ready for. "As much as I'd like to get you to myself in a dark theater, we better not."

"What do you do on the weekends?" he asked.

She shrugged. "Sometimes I'll study, and sometimes I'll shoot pool with friends."

"Are you any good?"

Hustler-good. She hid her smirk. "Above average."

"Pool it is, then." Rafe grinned and took the next exit off the freeway. "The dad of a kid I went to school with opened a pool hall and arcade for those who can't get into bars."

"Smart." Kallie nodded in approval.

"Yeah, it was. It's frequented by adults who don't want to shoot pool or play arcade games in a smoky saloon," Rafe explained.

Fifteen minutes later he turned into the parking lot of a fairly large gray stone structure with a familiar blue stripe. "He converted an old department store when they built their new supercenter about a mile away."

"I thought I recognized it."

"Would you like me to call some friends?" He draped an arm over her shoulder.

Kallie reveled in his warmth, his strength. She shook her head. "No. Let this be our date."

He grinned. "Yes, ma'am." He exited the car and hurried around to the other side, holding out his hand as he opened her door. "After you."

"Why, thank you kind sir." She deliberately stroked her hand along his jaw as she entered the building in front of him. His eyes darkened to emerald fire and he nipped at her finger when it grazed his lower lip.

Even at the end of November, the waning Texas sun was still intense, and Kallie took a few minutes to let her eyes adjust to the interior. The pool hall was well-lit, making sure all areas were safe, but it was still dim compared to being outside.

Rafe tucked her hand in his elbow. "I'll get you back for that," he growled softly. "But for now, follow me." He guided her through the throng of people and arcade games toward the rows of pool tables off to the left side. Along the right wall was a bank of pinball machines.

Kallie let him lead her as she looked around, taking in her surroundings.

The arcade was well-designed, from the position and selection of games to the lighting. Even the pool tables looked well-maintained. Kallie perused the racks along the wall next to the tables, the cues standing at attention like soldiers awaiting their orders. Each rack was coordinated by the weight of the cue. A sign hung above the racks in big blocky print. *Please return cues to proper racks.*

"Does anyone do that?" she asked.

"I do. So do most of my friends." Rafe selected his weapon of choice, a nineteen-ounce cue from two racks over. "The owner has enough to deal with. Cleaning up after disrespectful teenagers shouldn't be one of them."

Kallie fell in love with him a little bit more. She grabbed the least-warped cue from a heavier set and they passed several people playing as they made their way to an open table nearby. Rafe put quarters in the slot and pushed in the tray.

The sound of tumbling billiard balls was music to her ears.

She moved to the end by the ball return and started placing the colored balls into the wooden triangle.

Rafe covered her hand with his. "What are you doing?"

She grinned. "I'm being nice, giving you the first rack." She quickly set the balls and tightened the rack, then placed the head ball over the dot and removed the triangle.

"Wow." He whistled low. "I'm impressed."

"What? That I can properly set a rack of billiard balls?" Kallie snickered. "Honey, you ain't seen nothin' yet."

"Should I be worried?" he asked, lining up the cue ball for the break. "You're not gonna hustle me or anythin', are you?"

Kallie laughed outright. "No, Rafe. I'm not gonna hustle you."

His shoulders lost their tension as he leaned over the table for his breaking shot. She leaned against the wall, admiring the way his jeans stretched over his thighs. With one smooth thrust of the cue, he sent the cue ball across the table. The balls ricocheted across the green felt, but none dropped. The black eight ball rolled to a stop against the point of the left-side pocket; one light tap in the right spot would make it fall.

"Tough break." Kallie chalked her cue and lined up for her first shot.

Deliberately, she chose a ball that would put her on the opposite side of the table from him. The neckline of her shirt dipped as she leaned over, giving him a glimpse of her cleavage. He shifted his stance, revealing the effects she was having on him. She smiled. *Message received.*

She drew the smooth maple shaft across her fingers and gave it one sharp thrust. The satisfying thud of the red three-ball sinking into the pocket rang in her ears. The cue ball had drawn back perfectly, resting in an open area in the center of the table. She surveyed the layout, and smirked.

Her next shot put her on the same side of the table where he stood. She sashayed over and bent over the table, giving him a good view of her backside. She wiggled her hips slightly as she set the cue and took her shot.

"I know what you're tryin' to do, darlin'," he said.

Straightening, Kallie turned and propped her hip against the table. "I have no clue what you mean." She tried to sound innocent, but her voice came out breathless with desire.

He closed the distance between them, his footsteps slow and measured. "Care to put a wager on the game?" His gaze blazed with answering passion, his lips a hair's breadth from hers. "I'm sure I can think of a suitable forfeit."

"That's okay." She knew her skill, and it wouldn't be a fair fight. "Maybe next time I see you."

Turning to the table, her backside brushed against his front as she set her stance. She sank her next three balls, drawing the cue ball back to the open center after each one. The green six-ball rested near the black eight. That move was the toughest on the table, and she chose it as her next. She called on every ounce of her experience as she sent the cue ball into the six. The green ball kissed off the eight, knocking the black ball slightly off-center and away from the pocket as the six sank cleanly.

"Oh, wow!"

"Nice shot!"

"Can you teach me that move?"

Kallie looked up. Six teenagers were watching from the sidelines. "Sorry, boys. I don't give lessons." She'd forgotten they weren't alone in the arcade; she'd been so focused on Rafe and their game.

"You should," one of them said. He couldn't be any older than sixteen. "You're great!"

She smiled. "Thank you."

Conscious of the growing crowd, she sunk her final two balls, then called the eight in the opposite corner from where she could easily knock it in. She couldn't help showing off her skills.

"Don't you want to put it in that pocket?" Rafe asked. "If you miss, there's no guarantee you'll get another turn."

Kallie bit back her grin. "I'll take my chances."

She bent over the table and lined up for the bank, giving him another glimpse down her shirt. The black eight-ball bounced perfectly off the rail and rolled straight into her called pocket.

"Two out of three," Rafe said.

Kallie laughed. "Up to you. I'll even let you break again."

He chuckled, sliding quarters into the slot. She set the rack and sat on the stool next to the table, sipping water from the bottle he'd taken the liberty of ordering during the last game. The cool liquid soothed her parched throat and her overheated body.

His curse brought her attention back to the table, just in time to see the cue ball trail behind the eleven.

She chuckled. "Problems, dear?"

"Your turn."

"I gathered." She picked up her cue from where it rested next to the table and, with a coy glance at him, slid the smooth wood through her palm. His breath hitched and desire made his eyes sparkle.

He strode to the table and rested his cue against the bar stool, then wrapped her in his arms. "You're playin' with fire, darlin'."

She drew her finger down his arm. "Am I?"

He growled at the contact and he pressed her closer to him. She could feel the evidence of his desire against her hip. "Don't start somethin' neither of us is ready to finish."

His warning was clear. She reveled in the knowledge that she affected him as much as he affected her, but she backed off. Of course, neither of them were ready to take that next step. "I believe it's my turn."

Without a word Rafe let Kallie go. She took another long pull from the water bottle, then played out her turn at the table.

A few hours later Kallie snuggled into Rafe on his front porch swing.

"You said you were only above average," Rafe said. "You hustled me, darlin'."

Kallie smiled into his shoulder. "Yeah, I guess I did." She looked up at him, her expression sobering. "But I don't play to cheat anyone, and I never play for money."

"So, how did you learn to play that well?" he asked in a neutral tone.

She met his gaze, and only saw curiosity. "I had a lot of time on my hands, so I spent it studying the nuances of the game." She shrugged. "It's no different than you wanting to play better baseball."

He was silent for a long moment. "I suppose that's true."

"Can we talk about something else, please?" she asked to draw attention away from her pool skills.

"Sure." He kissed the top of her head. "What do you want to talk about?"

Instead of answering his question, she leaned up and kissed him, telling him with her lips what she couldn't quite put into words. When Rafe broke off, they were both breathing hard. His fingers threaded into the hair at her nape as he rested his forehead against hers.

Kallie closed her eyes and reveled in the heat that was Rafe Donaldson. She wouldn't think about leaving in the morning just yet.

Chapter 12

Rafe stretched out on the weight bench, pressing a barbell with seventy-five pounds secured to either end of the bar. Kallie's image appeared to project onto the ceiling above him, pushing him on, encouraging him to go for his dreams.

Except, his dreams had changed. He still wanted to play pro ball, but now he wanted a future with his Kals. They'd talked often as the fall semester finals approached, and he knew he'd never tire of hearing her soft, melodious voice.

"Come on, man," Callan said from the spotter's position. "Get your head together."

Kallie's image disappeared as Rafe pushed up the bar, his chest burning.

"Wimp," Callan heckled. "One more, Shrimpie."

"Shut up," Rafe growled, shoving the bar over his head again.

"One more," Callan demanded, cupping his hands beneath the weight as Rafe lowered it to his chest.

"Argh!" he grunted, lifting the bar one final time.

Callan helped Rafe set it back into the safety rack. He sat up and snagged a towel from the floor, wiping his face. He panted hard, his whole body burning from exertion.

"Dude, I've seen you do twice as many reps with that weight." Callan sat on the bench next to him. "What gives?"

"Nothing," Rafe said from behind the towel.

"Is it Kallie?" Callan asked softly.

"No." Rafe shook his head, lowering the towel. "Not really."

Though during their last conversation three days ago, he'd been left with the impression that she was distancing herself from him. They hadn't talked as long, and she'd sounded distracted. Like she couldn't get him off the phone fast enough.

Callan broke the silence. "What about the majors?"

Rafe met his teammate's eyes. "Nothing's changed there."

Three teams were still interested in him, and he'd been in regular contact with their scouts.

"But you want it all."

"Yeah." Rafe sighed. "I guess I do."

"You'll make it, bro." Callan clapped Rafe on the shoulder. "As much as you love her, you'll make it."

His teammate's words, and Kallie's image, carried him through the rest of their workout. He showered and changed in record time, anxious to get back home so he could call her again. He needed to hear her voice, desperate to know she still wanted him as much as he wanted her.

Rafe's long stride carried him quickly across the parking lot. Popping the trunk on his beat-up Taurus, he dropped his bat bag on the carpet. The duffel landed next to it. After slamming the lid closed, he unlocked the door and slid behind the wheel. He dug his phone from his pocket and scrolled through his contacts, tapping Kallie's name when it appeared on the screen. His fingers drummed the wheel as he waited impatiently for her to answer.

Her voice mail kicked in moments later. He disconnected without leaving a message, his heart sinking. Jamming the key into the ignition he started the car and headed home.

Thirty minutes later he pulled into the driveway and parked next to his mom's ancient Neon. Emptying the trunk, he hauled his gear into the house through the utility room. He dropped the duffel on the floor next to the washing machine and kicked off his shoes, then headed upstairs.

"Rafe?" Mom called from her bedroom down the hall. "Is that you?"

"Yeah." He set his bat bag on the floor in front of his closet and strode to her room. "What's up?"

Mom hung a load of shirts in her closet and closed the slatted bi-folding doors. "I'll need your help with supper tonight."

"Sure." He followed her back downstairs to the kitchen.

Ten minutes later Mom was chopping vegetables at the counter and Rafe was at the table up to his wrists in chicken juice and seasonings when his phone vibrated in his pocket.

Groaning in frustration of possibly missing yet another of Kallie's calls, he finished prepping the meat and set it in the roaster. He washed his hands, then dug his phone from his pocket. Sure enough, it had been her. He slid the roasting pan into the oven then walked to the living room and onto to the sofa as his phone beeped. At the same time her voice mail greeting kicked in.

"Hey, Kals. It's me. I just wanted to hear your voice again –" He stabbed the end-call button, taking out his frustration on his phone. *Way to go, Rafe. She probably thinks you're a moron.*

Tapping the voicemail icon, he listened to her message. She apologized for missing him earlier, and said she'd be with Amy for the rest of the night.

Playing back the recording, he listened for any sounds of hesitation in her voice. Or signs that she may not want him anymore. But she was upbeat, and he got the impression that she was as anxious to hear back from him. Instead of calling her back again, he just sent a text saying to have fun and that he'd try calling her again tomorrow.

Mom poked her head around the corner of the wall. "Is everything all right?"

"Yeah, Mom. I'm good." *Well, almost.* "I missed Kallie's call." He briefly explained their current game of phone tag.

"I know you miss her." Mom sat next to him on the sofa. "You two will find a way to make it work."

Something had been nagging him since Kallie's visit three weeks earlier. "Mom, why were you so distant with Kallie when she first got here?"

"I hadn't met her, and you rarely talked about her." Mom sighed. "Every time I'd called you when you were in Wisconsin, you'd been distracted. You said it was just baseball, but I knew something was different. You were different." She smiled. "And when you asked if she could stay here over Thanksgiving, well...I suspected it was more. That this girl meant more to you than you'd been letting on." She patted his knee. "For the first time, my son asked me to meet his girlfriend, and I wasn't sure how to handle it."

A blush crept up his neck and he couldn't meet his mom's gaze. "I'm sorry."

"Don't be. I figured you'd tell me when you were ready."

Relief overtook him as he hugged her. "Thank you."

"Anytime." She held him close. "I love you, Rafe."

"I love you too, Mom." They let go and he leaned back into the cushions.

Mom ruffled his hair. "Let's go check on dinner."

Kallie sat at a table on the second floor of the La Crosse Public Library, her textbook spread open. But she couldn't concentrate. In the two days since Rafe's last voice message, she still hadn't heard his voice, though they'd texted often.

Between finals and picking up shifts at the salon to cover for the groomers who'd wanted extra time off over Christmas break – her agreement from when she'd taken off work on short notice to visit Rafe for Thanksgiving – she hadn't had much time to herself. Her honors GPA had taken a hit, with her dismal spring semester and passing all of her fall classes with Bs and Cs.

She fixed her gaze on the quilt hanging from the rail above the stairs, the colors blurring in her vision. She closed her eyes and took a deep breath, clearing her mind. When she opened them again, Amy sat opposite from her.

"How's the studying going?"

"Better than last spring." Kallie set down her pen, giving up the pretense of concentration. "I'm just having trouble with this last class."

"What's causing the distraction?" Amy asked. "The class? Or Rafe?"

"To be honest, probably both." Kallie sighed. "We've been trying to talk to each other for the past two weeks, but we can't seem to do more than text."

"Do you still love him?"

Amy asked the question quietly, but it echoed like a shout in Kallie's ears. Her head came up and she met her friend's gaze. "With all my heart." She clasped her hands together over her homework. "I've never cared so deeply about a guy before." If she never heard from Rafe again, it would hurt. A lot.

"It isn't always going to be like this." Amy rested her hand on Kallie's arm. "You've told me over and over that you and Rafe have separate paths. It's gonna take work and trust, but it'll happen. Just have patience. You'll be together again."

Tears blurred Kallie's vision. She knew she'd always have Amy's unwavering support. But she hadn't realized how abiding their friendship was. "Thanks, Ames. You're the best."

"I know."

Kallie chuckled as she wiped her eyes.

Amy grinned. "Just name your first kid after me."

A huge weight lifted from Kallie's shoulders as she smiled back at her friend. "Come on. Help me pass this last final."

With a lighter heart and a clearer mind, Kallie studied with Amy for the rest of the night. The announcement that the library was closing was the only indication Kallie had of how long she'd been there. Packing away her books, she again thanked Amy for always being there for her. As they descended the stairs to the first floor near the circulation desk, their conversation returned to Rafe.

When they stepped outside Kallie discovered she and Amy were parked on opposite ends of the dimly lit lot, and she was closest to the library entrance. She unlocked her truck. "Get in. I'll give you a ride."

"My car is just over there," Amy protested.

"As dark as it is, you could get mugged. And it would be partly my fault because I let you."

"Kallie, don't be ridiculous," Amy scoffed.

Kallie glared at her friend. "Get in the truck."

"You sound like my mother," Amy huffed as they both climbed into the pickup.

Kallie started the motor and drove to where Amy's car was parked beneath a burned-out street lamp. Glancing in the mirror, she thought she saw something move in the shadows by the fence. The overgrown weeds rustled, and a squirrel darted up the tree. Breathing a sigh of relief, she turned to Amy. "I'll see you in class tomorrow."

"Yep." Amy hopped to the ground and shut the door.

Kallie made sure her friend was safely in her car before driving away.

Two days later Rafe started at the ceiling as he lay in bed, his fingers laced beneath the pillow. The clock read nearly eleven-thirty. His mom had gone to bed an hour ago. He should be asleep too, since he had to be up early for his last exams of the semester, but his thoughts raced a thousand miles an hour. Doubt had wormed its way into his heart and he couldn't seem to shake it.

He rolled onto his side and turned on the bedside lamp, then grabbed his phone and pulled up his messages to Kallie. He needed to hear her voice, even just for a few minutes.

His thumbs flew across the touch pad. *You still awake?*

Moments passed. His phone stayed silent.

Minutes later she still hadn't replied. He set his phone back on the table and flicked off the light. He lay on his back and pulled the blankets up to his chest, then closed his eyes. He controlled his breathing by counting with his heartbeat, hoping to calm his thoughts. Just as he was on the edge of sleep, his phone beeped.

The screen a perfect nightlight, he snatched it with his fingertips, but instead it clattered to the floor. Half-rolling off the mattress, he picked up from where it slid beneath the bed. Punching in the security code, he cued up her text.

Just got your message. Was shooting pool with Amy.

Rafe couldn't stop the grin from splitting his face. *She must be a glutton for punishment to take you on.*

The icon flashed. He held his breath waiting for her reply.

LOL. No, she's almost as good as me.

He was about to reply when a second message appeared moments after the first. Damn, she was fast.

I taught her everything she knows. (wide grin emoji)

He laughed. *She must be good.*

She has to be, to keep up with me.

I bet. Having been on the receiving end of Kallie's pool skills, he could only imagine how well Amy played. But he didn't want to talk about her friend. *Is it too late to call?*

He'd phrased the request as a question, hoping she wouldn't pick up on how desperate he was to talk to her. His phone went silent. The icon didn't even blink. Three minutes passed. Then three more. When she still hadn't replied after ten, his heart sank. Cursing himself a fool, he set the phone back on the nightstand. *She probably knows you're desperate to hear her voice.*

He punched his pillow in frustration with both his head and his fists. Just as he'd gotten settled, he heard the special song he'd chosen as the ringtone for when Kallie called him.

Bolting upright, he reached for the phone. Only, he caught it with his fingertips. It landed on the floor again. He threw back the blankets, snagged the device from the carpet, and swiped his thumb across the screen. "Hey beautiful."

"Hey handsome. What are you wearing?"

His heart leapt into his throat. Did she really ask him that? "Oh, I'm in bed." He sidestepped her loaded question. "Did you have fun tonight?"

"I did." She paused. "I miss you."

"I miss you too, Kals." His pulse slowed from hearing her voice. "How are finals going?"

"Better than last semester. As long as I get A's in four of my five classes in the spring, I'll still graduate with Honors."

Rafe rolled onto his side, the phone between his ear and the pillow. "That's great."

"What about you?" she asked. "How's practice going?"

"Haven't started team drills yet." He smiled. "But I've been strength-training and conditioning with Callan."

"I suppose, start early to get an edge on the other guy."

Rafe chuckled. "Something like that."

"How are your classes going?"

"More challenging than I'd anticipated. But they're fun, and I'm learning a lot." He'd been learning how to handle the business side of baseball, and to spot when an agent was trying to take advantage of him.

"Any news on the scouting front?" She asked the question lightly, but he heard something else in her voice. A note he didn't dare define.

"About the same," he replied, keeping his tone casual. "Contingent on how well I do this spring."

The thought of throwing the season just to be with Kallie had crossed his mind, but he'd decided against it. His mom still worked two jobs to stay afloat, and he was determined to make sure she wouldn't have to do it for much longer. He wouldn't just be hurting himself. He'd be hurting his mom too.

"Of course." Kallie cleared her throat. "I hope you make it, Rafe. I have every faith that you will."

"Thanks, darlin'." Now he just had to deliver.

"Anytime. Even though I won't always be in the stands, I'm always cheering you on."

The smile in her voice made him smile again. "I'm glad." He couldn't help the powerful emotions overwhelming him. "I love you, Kals." He couldn't let another moment pass without telling her.

"I love you too, Rafe." She giggled. "Maybe next time I see you, you'll be in the uniform of a *professional athlete*."

The way she'd drawn out the words made him chuckle, though he hoped he'd see her before then. Who knew how long it'd take him to reach the top, but he admired her conviction. Despite the niggling of doubt in his head as they rang off, his heart believed.

Rafe flicked on the lamp and attached the phone to the charging cord plugged into the wall beneath the nightstand. He set the phone next to the lamp, then flicked off the light. Plopping back onto the pillows, he stared at the ceiling for a few moments, a smile on his lips. Rolling onto his side, he inhaled deeply through his nose, then closed his eyes and released the breath through his mouth. His whole body relaxed as he drifted off to sleep.

Chapter 13

Five months later Kallie sat on the sofa in her parents' living room, the live broadcast of the baseball draft playing on the fifty-inch big screen. Rafe's name still hadn't been announced after five rounds. Though Rafe's Loggers teammates David, Callan and Justin had already been chosen for various teams. David was picked by Tampa Bay, Callan by Colorado and Lucas by Pittsburgh.

"You've never cared about any sports draft before." Olivia plopped onto the sofa next to Kallie. "What's so special about today?"

"I'd never known any of the players that could get drafted," Kallie replied. "My boyfriend could have his name called today."

It would change things between them, she realized. If he didn't make it, he'd have to really sell his resume to get teams interested. He'd have to get a regular job to pay bills while he waited for a team to pick him up.

Or, she thought, opting to remain positive, he'd get picked up right away.

A new worry gnawed at her. What if he was drafted, only to get cut after a season or two and have to start all over?

"What will you do if he gets drafted by San Francisco?" Mom handed Kallie a bowl of popcorn.

Kallie stuffed a few fluffy kernels into her mouth and chewed thoughtfully for a moment. "Probably wait for him to get established. Depending on where their rookie team plays, he probably won't start out in California."

"Have you applied to any research hospitals?" Mom asked.

"Not yet." Kallie had looked into every research opportunity available for her degree since January. She'd narrowed her focus to cancer research hospitals in Madison, Memphis and Baltimore, but she'd realized she'd have to take what she could get when the jobs became available. "I have an interview with Gundersen next week."

"I hope you don't move too far away." Olivia snagged some popcorn from the bowl between them. "We'll never see you again."

"Don't be so dramatic, Livvie," Mom said. "It's not like she'll be moving to a different country."

Kallie snickered. Olivia stuck out her tongue. Another team was about to announce their pick on the television. Kallie looked up, just in time to see the announcer. She held her breath. Rafe's name wasn't called. Disappointment rushed through her as she exhaled. Too restless to sit and too nervous to watch, Kallie walked to the door and put on her running shoes. "Let me know how it goes."

She stepped out into the humid late-spring air and did a quick stretch, then her brisk stride carried her on her way. Though the calendar had just turned to June, the air temps were already in the low eighties. She was halfway down the block when she'd realized she forgot her phone. Retracing her steps, she headed back to the house.

Seconds later her sister called out to her. "Rafe's on the phone for you."

Kallie dashed back into the house, giddiness bubbling inside her. Her mom handed her the cordless moments after she pushed open the front door. "Hello?"

"Hey, beautiful," Rafe's sexy drawl greeted her.

Kallie smiled, love blossoming in her heart. "Hey, yourself."

"Are you watchin' the draft?"

"My mom and sister are." Feeling a little winded, she bent at the hips and gulped in a lungful of air. "Why did you call my parents' number instead of mine?"

"I tried. You didn't answer. Are you okay?" he asked. "You sound out of breath."

"I'm good." Kallie plopped onto the sofa. "I was out for a walk when my sister told me you called."

"I'm glad she called you back. You didn't miss it."

Kallie sat up, instantly alert. "Miss what?"

"I have a feeling I'm going in this round."

She frowned, confused. "But San Francisco already selected their pick."

"I know," he said. "I've already agreed to a contract of sorts, so it's merely a formality."

"That's wonderful!" she squealed with delight. "Who did you sign with?"

"Keep watchin', darlin'."

She pouted. "You're really not going to give me a hint?"

He chuckled, the sound warming her insides across the line. "Nope."

"Jerk," she mumbled, and he laughed again. She'd never get tired of hearing that sound.

The next team was about to make their selection, and Kallie turned back to the screen.

The announcer stepped up to the dais. "Milwaukee selects Rafe Donaldson as their next pick for this year's draft."

"Omigod, Rafe!" Kallie couldn't contain her excitement. "Milwaukee!"

He laughed. "Surprise, darlin'."

"Where will you start first?" she asked, still flying high for him.

"With the rookie team. With luck I'll move up from there."

She heard him talking to someone in the background, before he returned to the line.

"I have to go, darlin'. I love you."

"I love you, too, Rafe." She wanted to hug him. "Congrats again, and good luck!"

"Hopefully I'll be able to get some of those lucky kisses from last year to help me along."

"Maybe," she teased. "Take care."

He disconnected a moment later. Kallie stared at the dead receiver in her hand, equal parts elation and disbelief washing through her. "Milwaukee," she said. "He's gonna play for Milwaukee."

"Awesome!" Olivia hugged her. "He'll be close to home."

"He'll start on their rookie team, then move up through the ranks." Kallie knew she should be excited about the prospect of Rafe playing in her home-state, but she couldn't help worrying about what his life would be like in the minors. Having seen how girls swooned over athletes in college, she wondered if he would even want her at the end of his journey.

Mom hugged her. "That's wonderful, dear."

It was. Adrenaline surged through her again. "I think I'll take that walk after all."

Dashing to her bedroom upstairs, she snatched the phone from her desk, the screen blank. It stayed dark when she tried turning it on.

"Oh, for Pete's sake." She plugged it into her portable charger and let it power up for about ten minutes, then tucked both into her pants pocket and popped in some ear buds before tuning in a music app on the device.

The route she chose was hilly, giving her a good, heart-pumping workout to burn off the excess energy racing through her blood. The exercise also helped clear her head. *Three years.* He'd spend three years in the minors honing his skills, then move up to the big leagues.

Suddenly three years seemed like a long time.

Two weeks later Rafe walked into the clubhouse at the stadium in Phoenix, not knowing what to expect. But the glares of animosity caught him by surprise.

A swarm of bees buzzed in his gut as he walked through what felt like a gauntlet to his locker on the other side of the room. Two jerseys hung on a hook in the open cubby, his name embroidered on the back.

"Don't get too comfy, rookie," his new teammate sneered. "You're not gonna be around long enough."

"I don't plan on it." Rafe tipped his cap and unloaded his gear.

Coming onto the team mid-season was always rough for everyone involved. He was the wrench thrown into the cogs of the wheel. But all he wanted was a chance to prove he belonged.

"What's that supposed to mean?" the guy demanded.

Rafe smiled with more confidence than he felt. He hadn't anticipated a confrontation within his first five minutes. "It means that I plan on moving up as quickly as I can."

The teammate smirked. "Yeah. You and every other guy in here."

"Hey, Larson," another voice shouted. "Lay off the new guy." The man had a mop of bright red hair and clear blue eyes, and held out his hand. "Noah Anderson. Welcome to Rookie Camp."

"Rafe Donaldson." Rafe accepted Noah's handshake. "How long have you been here?"

"Since the start of the season. Don't worry about Larson." Noah grinned. "His bark is worse than his bite."

"Thanks."

Noah shoulder-punched Rafe and walked to his own locker.

Rafe glanced at the jerseys one more time as he finished rearranging his stuff. Seeing his name and number on the back finally made it real. He was actually there!

Just as he'd reached for his phone to send a picture to Kallie, Noah chuckled behind him.

"You gonna suit up, rookie?" he asked. "Or are you gonna make love to it?"

"Sorry." Rafe grinned sheepishly, putting his phone back in his bag. "I'm still in shock, I guess."

"Don't worry about it," Noah said. "Many first-timers have that same reaction. It'll wear off soon, though. See you out there."

"Thanks, man." After a quick glance at Kallie's photo in his bat bag, Rafe changed into his uniform quickly and followed the tunnel to the dugout, ready to start his career in professional baseball.

He watched the other players – his new teammates – for a few minutes, trying to gauge their personalities. The first baseman waved at him from across the infield. He looked a little familiar, but Rafe couldn't immediately place him. Pushing the thought aside, he jogged out to the spot between second and third base to start his first practice.

Twenty minutes later the field manager called Rafe back to the dugout.

"Donaldson!" the coach bellowed.

Rafe jogged over to the dugout from his position at shortstop, confused why he'd been called out on his first day. "Yeah, coach?"

"Have you always played short?" Coach was about five-feet-six with shaggy brown hair and shrewd gray eyes.

"Yes, sir." Since Little League when Rafe had shown speed and a natural ability to field the ball.

"With your speed, I'm putting you in center."

"I'll do my best, coach."

"Larson!" Coach hollered to the center-fielder, waving in the other player to the dugout.

Howie Larson sprinted from the outfield back to the dugout. His grin turned to a scowl when he spotted Rafe. "Yeah, Coach?"

"Move to right. Rafe's gonna try center."

"But sir –" Howie protested.

Coach held up a hand. "Do it."

Apparently, the other player knew not to argue with the field manager. Rafe took his cue from his teammate and hustled out to center field. Setting his stance, he focused on the batter. The pitching coach lobbed balls and the hitter sent them flying.

Rafe got a bead on them and chased them down as best he could. He even managed to snag a few in the air. He had followed one into right field territory when he'd realized Howie hadn't even made a play for it.

The ball bounced off the fence behind them.

"You should have had that," he called to his teammate.

"That's what they got you for," Howie retorted.

Shaking off the insult, Rafe reset his position. Just in time to chase – and catch – another fly ball hit in the opposite direction.

Winded, Rafe felt like he'd been run ragged by the time Coach called him in for batting practice. When he got back to the dugout, he braced his hands against his knees and took a couple of deep breaths before grabbing his bat and jogging to the plate.

As he did with every at-bat, he drew DS in the dirt with the knob of his bat. On impulse, he added KH right next to it. Somehow, Kallie's initials looked like they belonged next to Dustin's. Like she was there cheering him on as much as his former teammate.

Rafe set his stance and awaited his first pitch. Connecting with the barrel of the bat, he sent the curveball deep to right field.

Howie Larson chased it, but it hit the wall over his head.

Rafe reset his stance, ready for the next pitch. This time he sent a grounder to short. The ball bounced between the player's legs and rolled into shallow left field before the player scooped it up and threw it back to second-base.

Rafe reset for the next. And the next. His turn at the plate lasted for about ten minutes. His arms felt like Jell-O and his bat weighed a ton. The batting coach signaled first base, so Rafe dropped the bat and sprinted up the baseline. After a few seconds, he ran to second, then third. The third-base coach waved him into the dugout.

"Hey, Rookie," Noah high-fived him, "not bad for your first day."

"Thanks." Rafe chugged some water from the nearby cooler and plopped onto the bench to watch the rest of practice.

"Larson's pissed." Noah sat beside him.

"I could tell." Rafe had a feeling he and Noah would get along just fine. Howie Larson on the other hand, would be more likely to bash his head in with a bat. "Not my fault if the coach wants to make a change."

"I know." Noah spat into the dirt. "He considers himself the team captain, though that job has already been assigned to the first-baseman, Justin Ellefson."

Why did that name sound familiar? Rafe looked over to where the first baseman was talking with the coach. Sure enough, it was the same Justin he'd played with last year in La Crosse. How had Rafe missed him when he stepped onto the field at the beginning of practice?

"Justin's a good guy," Noah said. "Been with us since last August or September."

"I know him," Rafe said. "He and I played for the Loggers last summer in the Northwoods League."

Thinking of La Crosse made him think of Kallie, and a pang of longing pierced his heart. *How soon will I see her again?*

"Oh, right. I've heard of them." Noah scratched his short beard. "They do a top-notch summer program."

Rafe nodded in agreement.

Noah pointed to the team's key players. "They're all rookies," he said. "But these guys have been here since day one of the season."

Including the aforementioned right fielder.

Did the coach sense a rivalry and had already decided to pit Rafe against Howie? Rafe couldn't help but think so.

He shrugged. "I guess we'll have to see how the season goes."

Eight weeks after Rafe had started playing Rookie Ball, Kallie scoured the minor league websites in search of his stats for the season.

They'd talked several times a week for the first month after he'd moved to Phoenix – usually during his off days – but their calls had tapered off and they'd texted more than they'd talked.

She'd let him know she'd landed her interview and was working at one of the hospitals in La Crosse, and – following his stats on the team website – she called to congratulate him whenever the team won.

His last text was two weeks ago.

Kallie chalked it up to him being busy with his travel and game schedule, but she'd started to worry about whether they were still together. Yet she didn't want him to think she was a needy girlfriend, requiring constant assurances that they were okay and that he still loved her.

She'd searched the team website for game updates, but nothing had been reported since the team was down three runs in the bottom of the fourth inning, so she turned to Google. Just as she hit 'search', her phone rang.

Not bothering to check the caller ID, she answered. "Hello?"

"Hey, darlin'." Rafe's drawl carried through the connection.

She smiled. "Hey, yourself."

"Did you miss me?" he asked.

"Of course I did." Kallie closed the web browser. "But the closer you get, the better my aim is bound to be."

He chuckled. "I better watch my back, then."

"Your back is safe. Your backside on the other hand …" Kallie clamped her mouth closed. "Forget I said that. How's your season so far?"

He chuckled again, the sound deeper and sexier than his last one. "Yours isn't safe either, darlin'. My season's been goin' pretty good. I'm not in Phoenix anymore."

"What? Why? You haven't been –" She couldn't bring herself to finish the thought.

"No, darlin'. I'm still playin'. I've just been moved up to the next level. They shipped me to North Carolina for low-A three weeks ago, and my schedule's had me run ragged."

"That's a relief."

"Justin says hi, by the way."

"Justin?"

"Yeah. Justin Ellefson. He was in La Crosse with me last year."

"Oh, that Justin." Kallie vaguely remembered his former teammate, though she couldn't remember catching his last name. "Tell him I said hi back." She took a breath. "Why did you wait so long to call me?"

"I'm sorry, Kallie. It took a couple of weeks to settle in. But I got your texts, and I've been thinkin' about you every day." He exhaled a breath. "Congrats on your new job. I know that was one place you wanted to get into. Have you heard from the research hospitals?"

"I – I haven't sent an application yet."

"Why not? What's stoppin' you?"

"I just started working. I don't have enough experience to apply."

"Kallie, don't let the lack of experience hold you back. You owe it to yourself to at least try. I mean, the worst they can do is say no, right?"

She made a noncommittal sound. "I guess time will tell."

A burst of noise exploded in the background, like a group of people all talking and shouting at once.

"I'm sorry, Kallie. I have to go. I'll call you when I get settled in North Carolina, okay?"

"Okay. Good luck, Rafe."

"Thanks, Kallie."

"I love you."

But he already hung up.

Chapter 14

One month. Rafe growled in frustration and threw his glove into his bat bag. It had been one month since he'd last talked to his girl. They'd texted and played lots of phone tag, but that was it. When he was free, she was working. And vice versa.

Her image, which he carried everywhere, smiled back at him from where he'd tucked a photo inside the bag.

"Hey, Rafe." Justin sat on the bench next to him. "A bunch of us are going to the local watering hole. Wanna come?"

"Nah." Rafe shook his head. "I want to try and connect with Kallie."

"Still seeing her, huh?"

"Yeah." At least, he hoped they were still together even though all they'd done so far is play phone tag.

After today's win against one of the toughest teams in their division, Rafe should be riding high. Especially after he'd robbed the other team of a grand slam with two outs in the top of the seventh inning. But there he was, lamenting over not being able to share it with his girl.

Long-distance relationships suck.

"Well, you've made it this far together," Justin said. "You're obviously doing something right."

Before Rafe could respond, a door slammed, the sound echoing off the concrete walls.

"Yo, ladies," Howie Larson taunted. "You comin'? Or are you gonna spend the rest of the night braiding each other's hair?"

"Stuff it, Baby Face," Justin shot back.

Rafe finished loading his gear into his bag and zipped it up, not giving his teammate the chance to look at Kallie's picture. He stood, hoisting the bag onto his shoulder. "I'm gonna sit this one out. You guys have a good time."

As Rafe strode to the exit, he heard Larson sneer, "What bug crawled up his ass and died?"

Ignoring the insult, Rafe left the clubhouse and strode out to his car. Once he was behind the wheel, he dug his phone from his bag and hit the speed dial he'd set for Kallie.

Her voice mail kicked in moments later.

He hung up without leaving a message. Instead, he sent a text.

I miss you. It's been too long since I last heard your voice.

After sending the first one, he quickly typed another.

I want to see you again. What does your schedule look like? I want you at one of my games this season.

When no reply came within a few minutes, he dropped his phone into the cup holder and started the engine of his car.

Kallie read Rafe's text and tried calling him back. His voice mail kicked in, and she stabbed the "end call" button with more force than necessary without leaving a message. Instead, she responded with a text apology for missing his call and gave him a time when he could reach her better.

"Was that Rafe?" Amy looked up from where she was taking her turn at the pool table.

Kallie nodded. "We keep playing phone tag, and it's frustrating the heck out of me."

Amy took her shot, but the cue ball went wide and bounced between the points of the far corner pocket. "At least the distance forces you to communicate."

"When we actually connect." Kallie stepped up to the table and surveyed the layout before lining up her next shot. "Most of the time we text and miss each other's calls."

She sent the cue ball into the four, knocking it into the side pocket.

"Nice shot." The deep timbre of a man's voice resonated across the table.

Kallie looked up, and saw a man standing along the wall next to the tables. Even in the dim lighting she could tell his hair was golden-blond, and he was extremely good-looking. And older.

Dressed in jeans, cowboy boots and a polo shirt that stretched across the breadth of his wide shoulders, he looked like the type of guy that could make Kallie forget she had a boyfriend. Thankfully the moment didn't last long, and once again her thoughts centered on Rafe before returning to the game.

"Thank you." She took her next turn, sending the cue ball trailing after the seven.

"Smooth." Amy chuckled as Kallie returned to their table, keeping the object between her and the man.

"Where did you learn to play?" he asked.

"She's been playing most of her life," Amy replied for Kallie. "She got me interested a few years ago when we both started college."

The man nodded, a gleam of speculation glinting from his eyes.

Even this close, Kallie couldn't tell if they were brown, green or blue. Maybe hazel? Top Shots was too dimly lit for her to get a good look.

"Darn it!" Amy cried out from the table, drawing Kallie's attention back to their game. "I should have had that!"

Taking her time, Kallie checked the layout of the table before selecting her next object ball. The worn cue slid easily between her fingers as she sent the cue ball into the three, pocketing it easily into the far corner. Knocking out her two remaining object balls, she sunk the eight with a little more flair than usual.

"Good game," she said to Amy, who nodded in response.

"You've got some decent skills," the man said. "Mind if I play?"

"Sure," Amy replied, chalking up her cue.

Kallie leaned her cue against the table and reached for her phone again. "I'm gonna sit this one out. Have at it."

After the man, who'd introduced himself as Harley, set the balls, Amy lined up for the break.

Tuning out the game, Kallie checked her phone for more messages from Rafe.

Unfortunately, there were none.

She pulled up the team website where he'd been transferred to check his stats, but his name wasn't listed on the active player roster. She called his number again, but it went straight to voice mail.

"Hey, Rafe. I saw –" She broke off. "I hope everything is going well. I miss hearing your voice, too. I think I talk to your voicemail more than I talk to you. Anyway, have a good night, and I hope to hear from you soon. Love you."

She disconnected the call after leaving the message and set her phone next to her purse, then took a sip of the watered-down cocktail. Condensation rolled down the side of the glass, soaking the napkin on the table.

Her phone rang again, Rafe's number flashing on the screen. Glancing at the time, she noted that it was almost midnight on the East Coast. Grabbing her phone, she signaled to Amy that she was going outside.

Amy nodded as Kallie slid her thumb across the screen.

"Hey, handsome."

"Hey, gorgeous," he replied in his sexy drawl.

"I didn't expect a call back tonight."

"I couldn't wait another day to hear your beautiful voice."

While the street wasn't as loud as inside the bar, Kallie still had difficulty hearing him. "I missed hearing your voice as well."

"Where are you?" he asked. "It sounds like downtown Charlotte durin' a NASCAR weekend."

"Outside Top Shots. Amy and I are having a girls' night." She shifted the phone against her ear and walked around the corner to a quieter area. "How come you're up so late? How did your game go tonight?"

"We won." His voice held little enthusiasm.

"What's wrong, Rafe?" She furrowed her brow. "You should be on a high right now. This is what? Five in a row?"

"I should be," he conceded. "But I'm missin' my girl."

"Aww, you're so sweet." She leaned against the side of the building. "I'm missing my guy, too."

"Any chance you'll be able to fly to Raleigh for a game this season? I really want to see you."

"I'm sorry, Rafe. I'm just starting to get into the swing of my job, and I can't afford to leave right now."

"But I need to see you." His voice turned whiny. "Hold you. Kiss you."

"Don't beg," she teased. "It doesn't become you."

"Hey, Donaldson," a voice in the background jeered. "Don't be such a whiner."

Raucous laughter boomed across the line, but Rafe wasn't part of it. He wasn't amused, either.

"Friends of yours?" she deadpanned.

"Just my teammates," he replied, his tone nonchalant.

Kallie shifted against the wall. "Sounds like a good bunch."

"Some of them are." Rafe sighed. "Justin and Noah followed me from Phoenix to Carolina."

"That's awesome." Kallie remembered their conversation from when he was in Phoenix, about how he'd befriended the two players within the first week. "I'm glad you have some support there."

A chorus of "Rafe and Kallie sitting in a tree, K-I-S-S-I-N-G", followed by another round of bawdy laughter, filled the space between them.

Rafe cleared his throat. "I'm sorry, Kallie. You shouldn't have to put up with that."

The background noise disappeared.

"Don't apologize for those jerks," she said. "You're not responsible for their actions. They are."

"Still, it's late, and I've got another game tomorrow. Wish me luck?"

"Always, Rafe. Play great. Hit a homer for me."

He chuckled. "I shall do my best."

"Have a good night."

"You too, darlin'. Love you."

"Love you, too."

Disconnecting the call, Kallie went back inside the bar.

"Kallie!" Amy called out. "What took you so long?"

Kallie held up her phone as she walked toward their table. "Rafe called. I finally got a chance to talk to him."

"That's great!" She held up her drink. "This is Harley. He bought us another round."

Nodding, Kallie went to the table and set down her phone, eyeing the glass skeptically.

Amy approached, pool cue in hand. "Don't worry. I made sure our drinks were safe." She took a sip of hers to prove her point.

"Thank you." Though she knew it wouldn't help numb the ache in her heart, Kallie downed half the drink in one pull.

Fighting tears, she sat on the stool and waited for Amy and Harley to finish their game. Even through her frustration she could tell there was as much flirtation as shooting pool between her friend and the handsome man circling the table.

When Amy bent over to line up her next shot, she wiggled her hips. Harley sucked in a breath.

Kallie ducked her head and smiled. Apparently, her friend found a new beau. She looked up just in time to see Amy bank the eight ball into side pocket closest to her.

"That's game!" Amy called triumphantly, circling back to the table where Kallie sat.

"I call a rematch," Harley grumbled good-naturedly. "I think I just got hustled."

Amy laughed. "Nah. I just stepped up my game a little."

"In more ways than one, little darlin'." He placed his hand on her hip and drew her close to him.

Yep. Amy was definitely off the market.

"Want to play another?" he asked, addressing them both.

"Nah." Kallie finished her drink and grabbed her keys. "I think I'm gonna call it a night."

Tears pricked her eyes again as the emotional roller coaster of her long-distance relationship started taking its toll.

"Hey," Amy whispered. "Are you okay?"

"Fine." Kallie nodded. "I'm just tired. It's been a long day. But if you want to stay and spend time with Harley you're welcome to. Just make sure you text me so I know he's not a serial killer."

"No. We came together, we leave together. Girl code, remember?"

Kallie smiled at the pact they'd made their freshman year of college and started going out more. "Girl code. Of course."

Harley draped his arm around Amy's shoulders. "Are you ladies safe to drive?"

"I'm good." Kallie held up her empty glass. "This was my only one." Grabbing her keys and purse, she slid off the stool. "I'll give you a minute."

Appreciation and admiration flashed in Harley's hazel eyes as he nodded.

Amy gave him a sidelong glance. "Give me two."

"Of course. I'll be just outside."

As Kallie walked away from the table, she heard Amy and Harley exchange phone numbers. Apparently, they'd gotten to know each other while she'd been talking to Rafe.

The thought of him had tears rushing back to her eyes and the steps blurred in front of her as she descended to street level. How she managed to make it without tripping she'd never figure out.

Once outside she leaned against the building and breathed deeply as she tried to control her emotions.

How much longer can we go on like this?

The thoughts raced through her mind.

Could they hang on for another two years? Or longer, if that's what it took for Rafe to make it to the majors? What about her own dreams? She still wanted to go after a cancer research job. Did wanting her own future make her selfish?

She was no closer to answering those swirling questions when Amy emerged from the doorway.

If she sensed Kallie's inner turmoil, she never let on.

Instead, Kallie listened as Amy talked about Harley and how great of a guy he was. Though Kallie was alarmed to learn that he was ten years older than them, she chose to keep her concerns to herself. Glass houses and all.

Once she dropped Amy off at her parents' house, she drove back to her own.

Can we really have it all?

Or would time and distance eventually tear them apart?

Chapter 15

"What are you doing now that you're officially in the off-season?"

Rafe shifted the phone between his ear and the pillow. "I'm finding some work around here. I have a few job interviews lined up over the next couple of days."

"What? Why?" Kallie sounded alarmed. "You're a professional baseball player."

The reality of the minors had hit him after his first paycheck, which was barely enough to cover his portion of the rent on the house he'd moved into with Justin, Noah and another guy on the team. Not to mention a few meager groceries. When Milwaukee drafted him they'd given him a signing bonus equal to five years' pay as a rookie. Only the players who made it to the majors made the six-and-seven-figure salaries.

While he and his roommates hadn't had to play hungry, some of his teammates had.

"Sorry, darlin'. Minor leaguers don't make that much money, and it's only during the season while we're playing."

Though the promotion from Low A to High A at the end of this season would give him a bit of a pay increase, he still needed to pay bills in the off-season. Thankfully his scholarship had kept his college debts low and he didn't have the burden of student loans. Unlike some of the guys he'd played with in Phoenix.

"I'm still living with my parents," she said. "I could help you with some of your finances. Maybe send you some money for groceries."

"Kallie, no." As much as he appreciated her generous offer, his pride refused to let him accept it. "I'll be okay. I've made do with much less than what I have now."

Yet he'd still been blessed with what he had. For the first time in his life, he thanked the powers that be for a life as the son of a struggling single mother. His experiences as a child had given him better coping skills than some of his more well-to-do teammates.

"But I want to help. What if we got married? I'm sure I could transfer to a hospital in that area. Or, with my laboratory experience, I could work for GSK Pharmaceuticals."

This was the second time in as many months that she'd mentioned the M-word. He wasn't averse to it. Quite the opposite, in fact. But he didn't want her to suffer the stress and strain of him playing ball for basically peanuts and that was only during the five-month season. He couldn't put his finger on it, but something held him back from telling her about moving to Wisconsin next spring.

"I'm still gonna ask you to marry me, Kallie," he declared. "But not right now. I'm sharing a four-bedroom house with three other guys because none of us can afford anything else on our own. It's like a zoo around here. High testosterone all the time. I won't subject you to that."

Especially with his teammate's penchant for spending ninety percent of his time at home almost completely in the buff.

"Shouldn't I have a say in the matter?" she demanded. "I thought we were in this together, Rafe."

"We *are* in this together." A chill ran down his spine as he implored her to understand. "But us as a couple, living together with three other guys, is not the situation I want for either of us." He pinched the bridge of his nose. "I can't support you on my minor league salary, Kallie. And you shouldn't have to suffer living paycheck to paycheck in the off-season so I can train."

"There you go again, Rafe Donaldson. Making decisions for the both of us."

Her words knocked the breath from his lungs like she'd punched him in the gut. "Kallie, you've already sacrificed so much for me in the time that we've been together."

"It's not a sacrifice. I *want* to be with you. I can't wait the three years, or however long, it'll take you to get to the majors before I see you again. I can't."

The vehemence in her proclamation, and the knowledge that he'd be close to her next spring, made him grin. "Baby, you won't have to. Just keep doing what you're doing. Let me get through the hard part first, okay?"

"Fine," she conceded, though she didn't sound happy about it.

"I promise things will get better." He stifled a yawn. Not surprising, given the lateness of the hour and exhaustion setting in from his punishing workout that morning. "I love you, Kallie."

"I love you, too, Rafe."

As Rafe disconnected the call, he couldn't help wondering if they'd just had their first fight. They hadn't yelled at each other, but her accusation about him not giving her choices had hit too close to the mark.

He shifted onto his back and stared up at the ceiling in the darkened room, his thoughts drifting back to their conversation. If he did marry her now, he'd still be able to play ball during the summer, but what about the off-season? They wouldn't be able to live together on just her income alone, and he wouldn't expect that of her.

He'd seen the financial stress some of the other players' wives had to endure, just so their husbands could follow their dreams. Families put on hold or sacrificed altogether. Howie's wife was a teacher, and they lived on her salary alone for the five months he played ball.

Rafe didn't want that kind of burden for Kallie. She deserved far better than that. Some days he wondered if he was good enough for her, but he'd hear the love in her voice that made him aspire to be the man she deserved.

He wanted to take care of her, not the other way around. She'd accused him of making decisions for her. In his gut he knew he was right in asking her to let him do this part alone.

He was just protecting his girl from hardship. Right?

Kallie set her jaw. Come hell or high water, she would help Rafe achieve his goals. Never mind the fact that her own dreams kept slipping further away from her.

She'd reread the email she'd received from Baltimore more than once. They'd rejected her without even the courtesy of an interview.

Powering up her laptop, she Googled what life was like for minor league baseball players. The harsh reality that they didn't even make a livable wage during the season astounded her.

Going into her banking website, she looked at her last few paychecks and, after some quick math, realized she made more money in three months than he had during his entire summer of playing baseball. At least, according to the graphic on the website she'd found.

Exhaling a frustrated sigh, she closed the web browser and stared at the wall. Why did he have to be so stubborn about accepting her help? What was money compared to following dreams? Didn't he have faith that she'd support him in whatever capacity he needed?

Or was it more than that? Was he nursing wounded pride knowing she currently made more than he did? Didn't he realize that their current situation was only temporary?

For the first time since he'd told her about his dreams to play pro baseball, she acknowledged that the odds had been stacked against him from the moment he'd stepped onto the field.

That there was a very real possibility he'd never make it to the major level. What if he failed to achieve that ultimate goal?

What would happen to them if he didn't?

Fear snaked its way through her.

Would he walk away from her, too?

She couldn't imagine Rafe without baseball, just like she couldn't imagine her life without him.

Closing her eyes to stave off tears, she did her best to fight the voices of doubt whispering through her mind.

Have faith, he'd said. Be patient.

Sending up a silent prayer to whichever being was listening, she asked for a sign. Something to help her remain strong. Not only for herself, but for her boyfriend and their relationship.

Exhaling, she opened her eyes and glanced at the cork board above the desk in her bedroom. There, she saw a photograph of Justin, Rafe and David from when they'd played for La Crosse, next to one of just her and Rafe. The photos had been taken the night they'd won the Northwoods League championship. A night so full of elation and promise. The reward for a long, demanding season of grinding out every inning of every game.

"Okay, Rafe," she whispered. "For you, for our future, I will have faith and be patient."

Eight months later Rafe walked through the tunnel between the clubhouse and the dugout after his last game with Carolina. Tomorrow he'd be going back to Wisconsin, moving up from the Low-A team to High-A. In his world, that was a promotion.

So far, his second season in the minors was going better than his first. After a rocky start in Phoenix, he'd settled down and gotten into his groove.

Coach had moved him back from center field to shortstop after three games, acknowledging his natural agility in the infield, and helped teach him how to become a better shortstop.

Rafe had snagged the last line-drive ball in the air to win the game. Yes, he'd celebrated with his teammates, accepting the accolades of making the final out, but the victory seemed hollow. Like he had no one to share it with.

"Hey, Donnie Boy," Howie Larson called from behind him.

Rafe stiffened his spine and drew in a sharp breath at the derisive nickname. "What do you want, Larson?"

"Gonna come with us tonight and celebrate?" The other player waggled his eyebrows suggestively. "You look like you could use some female companionship, if you catch my drift."

"No, thanks." Ignoring the jibe, Rafe entered the locker room and stowed his gear, accidentally dislodging the photo of Kallie he'd kept tucked in there.

"What's the matter, Donny Boy? You gay or somethin'?" Larson picked it up from where it had fallen on the floor and gave a loud wolf whistle. "She's hot! Who is she? Your sister?"

"None of your business." Rafe reached for the photo, but Howie pulled it out of his grasp.

"She's gotta be your sister. Or maybe cousin. Yeah, that's it." Larson sneered. "Because she definitely looks too good for you."

Justin grabbed the photo and handed it back to Rafe. "Get out of here, Howie. Leave him alone."

"What the hell's your problem, man?" Larson chest-bumped Justin.

"Funny." Justin didn't back down. "I was about to ask you the same thing."

"Knock it off, boys!" Coach's voice echoed off the cinder block walls. "Larson. My office. Now."

"Have fun, ladies." Howie Larson spun on his heel and followed Coach.

But Rafe didn't miss the unmistakable glint of fear in the other man's eyes. He turned to his friend. "Thanks, man. I owe you one."

"It's all good." Justin grinned, hooking a thumb through his belt loop. "He's lucky I didn't lay him out."

Rafe chuckled. "That would've been somethin'."

Noah came over and hooked an arm around Rafe's neck. "I would've given anything to see that man flat on his back."

Rafe agreed. Howie had a wife, plus a kid on the way, yet he was always doing something to risk jeopardizing his baseball career.

Rafe glanced down at the photo he still held in his hand, remembering the last time he'd talked to Kallie. They hadn't had any more fights, but he could tell she was getting restless with the current status quo. Tucking it back into his bat bag, he finished storing the rest of his gear.

"She's beautiful," Noah said. "Who is she?"

"Her name is Kallie," Justin said, changing at his locker. "She's an amazing person, and they've been dating about two years."

Noah whistled as he moved to his own cubby. "You're a lucky man, dude."

"Don't I know it." Rafe hoisted the bag onto his shoulder. "See you guys at home."

Twelve hours later, Rafe had his meager belongings packed and was seated on the team plane headed for Appleton.

He'd adopted a minimalist lifestyle after one of his teammates in Phoenix had been shipped to Carolina three weeks after his arrival and ended up with three suitcases worth of stuff.

A team driver picked him up at the airport and drove him to his new home. The humid summer air made his skin prickle.

Grabbing his lone suitcase, Rafe walked into the front office entrance at the field.

"Rafe Donaldson." The field manager greeted him with a hearty handshake. "Glad you're finally here."

"We've heard some great things about you," the team owner said.

Rafe shook hands with the other staff members. "Thank you for giving me this opportunity."

They talked baseball for a few minutes, then the general manager took him into the stadium for a tour.

The last place they entered was the clubhouse, where Rafe was assigned his locker for however long he'd be there. A jersey with his name and number hung on a hook, yet the move up still didn't seem real.

"What about some of my teammates from back in Zebulon?" he asked. "There are a few who deserve this as much as I do."

"All in good time, Rafe," the GM said. "Practice is at three. Today's an off-day, so it'll be light duty."

"What about a place to live?"

"A couple of the guys are looking for another roommate. I'll put you in touch."

After a farewell nod, the GM left and Rafe looked around the clubhouse before stowing his gear in his cubby. Glancing at his phone, he had about an hour to kill before having to suit up.

Exiting the clubhouse and finding his way back to the grandstands, Rafe dialed Kallie's number. Surely, she'd be able to take a weekend off to watch him play now that he was so close.

"Hello?" she answered after the third ring.

"Hey, beautiful. It's good to hear your voice again."

"Likewise." Something rustled in the background. "It's been a week since I last received anything from you. Are you okay?"

"Yeah." He grinned. "I have some…news."

"Rafe, what is it?"

The alarm in her voice made him grin even broader.

"You haven't been cut from the team, have you?"

Even as she voiced his biggest fear, he chuckled. "No, darlin'. Nothin' like that."

"Then what is it? You're killing me over here."

"I'm in Appleton."

Her squeal of delight was so loud, he had to jerk the phone away from his ear. "Rafe, that's awesome! You're one step closer to your goal."

"That's why I'm calling." He glanced at his game schedule. "What does your schedule look like over the next couple of weeks?"

"Appleton is a lot closer than North Carolina. I should be able to take off a couple of days for a visit."

"I was hopin' you'd say that."

More rustling. "Let me coordinate my hours with your new game schedule and let you know in a couple of days, okay?"

"I miss you, darlin'. I can't wait to hold you again."

"I miss you, too, handsome."

They talked a few more minutes about nothing in general, before he hung up and returned to the clubhouse to get ready for practice.

When he stepped onto the field, his heart felt lighter than it had in over a year.

Chapter 16

Kallie stepped through the gates of the stadium in Appleton five days after receiving the call from Rafe. Her coworkers had been relatively sympathetic, and one of them gladly took her shift so she could make the drive.

Oh how I've missed him!

He'd left a ticket for her at the will-call counter along with one of his jerseys, which she happily slipped on over her t-shirt. As she made her way to her seat, she realized it was right up from third base behind the home team's dugout.

Would he be able to see her? How much had he changed since she'd seen him last? Would he see any noticeable changes in her?

An usher approached her. "Ms. Huntington?"

"Yes?" she replied.

"If you'll come with me, please? Someone would like to speak with you."

She followed him toward the front offices of the stadium and entered the open door he held for her. She entered the conference room, confusion knitting her brow.

Moments later the door opened again and Rafe emerged.

"Rafe!" She crossed the room and he wrapped her in a fierce hug.

"I can't believe that you're actually here. I couldn't wait until after the game to see you." He buried his face against her neck and held her for a moment before pulling back. "I need to claim my good luck kiss."

Kallie grinned. "Of course."

He cupped her cheek with his rough, callused palm and met her lips with his. She opened under the pressure of his mouth and he deepened the kiss.

When the pressure eased, her lashes fluttered and she met her gaze with his.

"Hi." His smile dazzled her more than she already was.

She smiled back. "Hello."

A knock on the door startled them apart. "Five minutes, Rafe."

"I guess that's my cue." He kissed her again, a quick brush of his lips against hers. "I'll see you after the game."

"I'd like that." She wrapped him in another hug.

He kissed her neck. "Did I mention how sexy you look wearing my number on your back?"

"Not lately," she murmured.

He snagged her arms and pulled away from her, then twirled her around. She giggled as his green eyes turned dark.

He finally put distance between them, like it pained him to do so, and nodded as he turned toward the door.

"Go get 'em, hon," she said, then watched as he walked out of the room, her eyes practically glued to his backside.

Before Kallie found her seat, she took advantage of the voucher the usher gave her for the concessions stand. Her seat straight up from third base gave her not only an incredible view of the stadium, but also of her handsome shortstop.

As Rafe moved around the infield, she studied his movement. Was it her imagination, or was his body more muscular than it had been the last time she'd seen him?

Granted it'd been two years, but he definitely looked good.

Had it really been two years since she'd seen him? He'd chosen to go back to Texas to spend the holidays with his mother. But she hadn't blamed him.

How much longer can we keep going on like this?

The answer whipped through her mind faster than lighting.

For as long as it takes.

Kallie pulled out her phone during the third inning and snapped a picture of Rafe at the plate. Zooming in on the image, she saw that he wore the same fierce expression that he had in La Crosse.

She almost wished she was on the first-base line so she could get a shot of his backside. Though she couldn't help admiring the view from this angle, either.

Being with him again felt right. Like the passing of time between their visits melted away and nothing else mattered except him and their future together.

The crack of the bat jolted her attention back to the game. She looked up, just in time to watch the ball sail into the stands for a home run.

Leaping to her feet, she cheered with the crowd as Rafe and his teammates cleared the bases and headed for home. Already up three-nothing, Rafe had doubled the score with one swing.

When he rounded third base, he pounded twice on his chest and then pointed to the section where she was. Almost as if he was telling her that he'd done it for her.

But how…?

Shaking her head, she laughed he crossed the plate and accepted the chest-bumps and high-fives by his teammates. Disappointment flittered through her when he disappeared back into the dugout.

The game ended with a Wisconsin victory. Kallie wondered where she was supposed to meet Rafe. She was almost to the main gate when someone wearing a team polo pulled her aside.

"Ms. Huntington, this way, please."

Kallie followed the portly man into a restricted area that led to what was called the clubhouse. She assumed it was the locker room.

She waited in an anteroom where she imagined players emerging from showers and getting dressed after nine exhausting innings on the field. Rafe would be one of them. Imagining him wearing nothing but a towel sent a surge of desire through her.

When he appeared fully clothed, she couldn't stop the disappointment from crashing through her. His slightly damp hair the only indication that he'd cleaned up.

"Hey, beautiful." He greeted her with a kiss. "Let's get out of here."

"Are you hungry?" she asked.

"Ravenous," he growled against her nape.

Shivers raced down her spine. Something told her his hunger had nothing to do with food. Which was fine with her.

"Cold?" he asked, fires of banked arousal burning in his green eyes.

"A little," she fibbed.

He wrapped an arm around her shoulders and guided her toward the exit.

"My, my," A male voice boomed behind them. "So the mystery girl is real after all."

Rafe groaned. "But out, Larson."

"Hell, Rafe," Howie Larson sneered. "For the way you kept ignoring all of the delicious ball bunnies, I thought you were gay."

"Not gay," Rafe countered, pulling Kallie close. "Just waiting for my girl. See ya tomorrow."

"Hey, gorgeous!" Larson yelled. "When you're ready to trade up, let me know."

The imp on Kallie's shoulder made her grin. Turning, she batted her lashes at the other player. "I already have, but thanks for the offer."

The look on the other man's face was priceless. Chuckling, he led her toward the player exit.

"What was that about?" she asked when they were outside.

"Nothin'," he said. "Smack talk between teammates."

Alarm bells went off inside her. "You talked about me to them?"

"Hell no!" He swore. "When I was playing for Carolina, he found a picture of you in my bat bag. He thought you were my sister."

Kallie chortled. "Oh, Rafe. That's too funny."

"I didn't think so at the time."

Of course he wouldn't. What he hadn't realized was that he'd just affirmed his feelings for her. The thought of him carrying her photo warmed her heart.

Stopping against a huge SUV, she wrapped her arms around his neck and pressed her body against him. "I love you, Rafe Donaldson."

His fingers dug into the soft flesh of her hips. "I love you too, Kallie Huntington." He kissed the tip of her nose.

"Where are you parked?" she asked.

He looked up and glanced around. "I, uh, actually came with one of my teammates."

"I was hoping I wouldn't have to follow you home." Guiding his head back to hers, she kissed him again. "Come on. My car is that way." She looked around the massive parking lot. "I think."

He chuckled. "I think I know where it is."

Grabbing her hand, he led her to the other side of the lot near the main entrance. Her car was the last one in her row.

The fans had wasted no time clearing the area while she'd been waiting for Rafe to come out of the locker room.

"Kallie? Which motel are you staying at?"

She gave him a puzzled frown. "I didn't book one. I thought – I was hoping to stay with you."

Groaning, he stowed his gear in her trunk. "And here I was hoping we'd be able to have some privacy."

She unlocked the car and they climbed in. "Rafe, what is it?"

"There's no easy way to say this." He shoved his hands through his hair. "I live with three other guys in a four-bedroom house."

"Oh." The humor of the situation made her laugh. "Well, I guess we'll just have to be quiet. Won't we?"

"God, Kallie." He laughed with her. "How did I ever find you?"

Though the situation wasn't ideal, she'd spent the night in his bed. Neither could afford a motel room. She'd already discovered that minor-league players didn't make nearly as much money as players in the majors, but now she was seeing it first-hand. His rented room was little more than the size of a pantry, and he slept on a queen-sized air mattress that took up almost the entire floor space. A coat rack in the corner served as his closet, and a small rolling cart next to it was his dresser.

What few toiletries he had were neatly arranged on top of the cart.

"Is everything okay, Rafe?" she gestured to the mattress.

"I know this isn't what you envisioned how a professional baseball player would live." He whisked his shirt over his head and hung it up on the coat rack.

Kallie could only stare at the male perfection in front of her, her mouth agape.

Chuckling, he strolled to the rolling cart and pulled out a pair of pajama bottoms, then shucked his jeans and pulled on the flannel.

"What's the matter, Huntington?" he teased. "Cat got your tongue?"

His fingers sliding through her hair snapped her from her trance. "Sorry. I didn't expect–"

"Life in the minors leaves no room for modesty." He kissed her gently, then pulled back the blankets on the mattress. "But if you insist, bathroom's down the hall on the left."

Grabbing her overnight case, Kallie decided that changing in the bathroom was probably for the best. She put on her jammies, ran a brush through her hair, then grabbed her case and returned to Rafe's room.

Sliding beneath the blankets, she turned onto her side facing him. "I can't believe you sleep on an air mattress."

"The minors are gruelin', darlin'." Rafe cradled her in his arms. "I'm playin' just about every day durin' the summer, and there've been times where my luggage hadn't caught up to me before I was bein' moved again. Let's get through the hard part first, okay?"

For the first time she understood what he meant when he'd said life in the minors was no picnic. "Just don't make me wait forever."

"I don't plan on it." His soft breath feathered her hair as his finger trailed up and down her arm. "How has work been going?"

"Good. My coworkers are awesome. They agreed to cover my shift so I could come here and be with you."

"I'm glad."

They talked for a while as they cuddled, her fingers curled into the packed muscle and sinew of his – bare – chest. One of his hands curled into the hair beneath her cheek, while the other rested on her hip.

Neither of them made a move to take their intimacy any further, though she was sure Rafe felt her racing pulse beneath his touch.

Silence settled around them as several hours of driving caught up with her. Kallie was just about to sleep when a loud slam crashed through the house. She'd have bolted upright, but Rafe's arms pinned her to the mattress. "What was that?"

Rafe groaned. "My teammates."

The clock on the rolling cart next to the wall read 1:57AM. "Do they always stay out this late?" she lamented.

"Not always." He pulled her close. "Must've been running high on adrenaline after the game."

Kallie reveled in his heat; his strength. "Do you?"

"Sometimes." He tried shrugging. "Not tonight, though."

"I'm glad."

The noise downstairs quickly settled, and Kallie tensed when she heard footsteps on the stairs. But no one bothered them in Rafe's room.

Closing her eyes, she drifted back to sleep.

The next morning Kallie decided modesty was overrated and changed in Rafe's tiny bedroom. Mostly she didn't want to get caught using the communal bathroom down the hall.

As she descended the stairs to the kitchen, the aroma of coffee hit her hard.

"I was wondering whose car that was parked outside," a male voice greeted her. "Hello, Kallie."

"Justin!" She recognized him from the last picture Rafe had sent her a few weeks ago. "I didn't know you'd be here."

"Yep." He puffed out his chest as he finished putting together his breakfast. "Just got called up from Low-A two days ago."

"That's awesome! Congrats!"

He blushed. "Thanks."

"Ellefson, quit flirtin' with my girl." Rafe entered the kitchen and wrapped his arm around her waist.

"Oh, she's got nothing to fear from me, old man." Justin grabbed his breakfast sandwich. "I'll just take this upstairs."

Despite the heat flaming her cheeks, Kallie laughed. "Do they think we –"

"Probably."

Mortification fused every cell in her body. "But we didn't!"

Rafe chuckled. "Don't worry about it, darlin'."

"What did Justin mean by 'old man'?"

"Nothin'." He shook his head, even as he grinned. "I'm a year older than him, which he thinks makes me ancient."

Kallie couldn't silence that impish voice inside her. "Well, I guess, in baseball terms, you probably are."

Reaching for her, he said, "I'll show you how old I am."

Giggling, she dashed to the other side of the room before he could grab her. But before she could get further, she crashed into someone else.

Two hands grabbed her arms. "Whoa there, little lady."

"Hands off, Noah," Rafe barked.

"Oh, you must be Kallie. Rafe's told us so much about you." Noah grinned, dropping his hands. "We didn't even know you were here last night."

Kallie returned to Rafe's side, a little disgusted by the unspoken innuendo in the other player's comment. "Not that it's any of your business."

"I'm kidding," Noah said. "It's nice to finally meet you."

"I wish I could say the same," Kallie said.

Noah put his hands up in surrender. "No harm intended. But had we known we'd be having company, I'd have made the boys clean up a little bit."

Kallie glanced around the mostly clean kitchen. "It's fine. I've lived with other girls before. I know things can get messy at times."

They chatted a bit longer while Rafe fixed them something to eat.

"I have to get to practice," he said after breakfast. "We won't have much time together before the game, but we'll go out for dinner afterwards, okay?"

Kallie nodded. She helped clear the table and wash the few dishes stacked in the sink, then went back to Rafe's room and grabbed her purse. Might as well get some sightseeing done, since she'd never been to this part of the state before.

Rafe kissed her before he and his teammates left for the field. Their catcalls made her face heat in embarrassment, but Rafe had no issues with PDA.

"I'll see you at the game, okay?"

Nodding, Kallie touched her fingers to her lips, still tingling with his touch. After they left, she got in her car and drove to the Fox River Mall to kill time.

She hadn't planned on buying anything while she was there, but the trinket in the window called to her. Minutes later she resumed her walk through the mall, her purchase in hand.

Now to plan when to give it to Rafe.

Chapter 17

Rafe stepped into the net for BP and set his stance as the hitting coach lobbed balls in his direction. After finishing his turn, he went back to the dugout.

Larson had given him a hard time when he'd gotten to the clubhouse, but he'd managed to shake off his teammate's derogatory comments.

Noah stepped onto the ledge next to Rafe and rested his forearms on the rail. "She's beautiful."

"She is." Rafe wondered why his teammate was bringing up Kallie now. Though she hadn't been far from his thoughts all day. Her warm, fragrant body snuggled next to his last night felt amazing. More right than anything had in his past relationships. "I think she's it for me."

"How long will she wait for you?" Noah asked, concern coloring his voice. "Many guys make it this far, but never get called up."

"I know." Again, Rafe kept his voice neutral. He never really talked about it, even with his teammates, but there was a very real possibility he would never make it out of the minors. "But I know she'll be there whether I do or not."

Noah looked out over the field. "Keep fighting, dude. You'll make it."

"That's the plan." But suddenly Rafe had a feeling he wasn't talking about baseball anymore.

That night's game was in front of a packed house. Rafe took the field for the first inning, glancing over where he'd gotten Kallie a seat up from third base. She was wearing his jersey again, which sent equal parts pride and desire rushing through him. She pounded her chest twice, then pointed at him. He grinned and nodded, then turned his eyes back to the batter's box and waited for the pitcher to start the game.

Afterwards Rafe was toweling off when Coach bellowed his name.

Dread filled his heart. There were only two reasons why a player got called into the office: they were being cut, or they were being moved up.

He fastened his jeans and grabbed a t-shirt, pulling it on as he made the long walk to the coach's office.

"Don't look so glum, Donaldson," Coach said. "We're sending you to Mississippi. You leave tonight."

"Mississippi?" Rafe asked in disbelief. "Tonight?"

"They want you there for tomorrow's game." Coach looked at him and frowned. "Is there a problem, Donaldson?"

"No problem, sir. But my girlfriend is in town. I was hoping to have more time with her."

A sympathetic gleam appeared in the older man's gray-green eyes. "I don't think we'll be able to get you another flight."

The meaning was not lost on Rafe. "Thank you for everything, coach."

They spent a few minutes going over the itinerary and accommodation. After shaking hands with the staff, Rafe went to his locker and packed all of his gear.

"Where are you going, Donny boy?" Larson sneered. "Get cut already? It's about damn time."

Smiling inwardly, Rafe kept his good fortune to himself. With any luck, Howie Larson would not receive the same. "Tough break, huh? Later, Larson."

Again Kallie waited for him outside the clubhouse. He looked at her – really looked at her for the first time since her arrival in Appleton – and his heart nearly broke.

Concern knitted her brow. "Rafe? What is it?"

He shook his head. "Not here. Let's go back to my place."

The drive back to his house was in silence. When they pulled up to the curb, she parked the car and killed the motor. "Rafe, you're scaring me. What is going on?"

"I'm sorry, Kals. I don't know how to say this."

"It's bad news, isn't it?" Sighing, she leaned back into her seat. "They're cutting you."

He took her hand, because he couldn't not touch her. "No, darlin'. They're not cutting me. They're moving me up to the next level."

"Rafe, that's great news!" She squeezed his hand. "When do you leave?"

He blew out a breath. Might as well rip off the Band-Aid. "Tonight. My flight leaves in two hours."

"Tonight? Are you sure?"

"I tried to get a later flight, but I couldn't. Kallie, listen. If I don't take this opportunity now, I may never get another one." The coach's words had been implied, but no less ominous.

"Oh." Kallie's face fell. "I get it. Congrats, Rafe. I know moving up is another step in the right direction."

"Don't be upset, Kallie." He knew he'd handled this badly and she was unhappy with him. "Like I said, life in the minors is no cake walk. I have to be ready to pack up at a moment's notice. Come inside with me?"

"Of course."

It took almost no time at all to deflate the air mattress and pack his meager belongings. He left the rolling cart and coat rack, but took everything else with him.

"Do you want me to drive you to the airport?" she asked.

"No, they're sending a car." An incoming notification made his phone vibrate and he glanced at it. "That's them now. Kallie, I wish –"

She crossed the empty room, wrapped her arms around his waist and leaned into his chest. "I know. So do I. But who knows? By this time next year you'll be in Milwaukee."

"That would be somethin'," he agreed.

"Call me, okay?" She rested her hand against his jaw. "Let me know when you get settled in Mississippi?"

He kissed her, unleashing all of the pent up frustration and passion he felt for this amazing woman. "Will do, darlin'."

His phone pinged again.

"Sorry, Kals. They're not waitin' on me. I gotta go."

After one last kiss, he grabbed his gear and went downstairs to meet his ride.

The two hours went fast. Before he knew it, he was in the air heading south. Rafe knew he should be elated that he'd been called up again.

But damn if he didn't feel like he was leaving even more of himself behind in Wisconsin.

Eyes bleary from a combination of crying jags and lack of sleep, Kallie turned into the driveway of her parents' house around four the next morning.

She'd planned to stay with Rafe for the entire series, but once he'd left for the airport there was nothing keeping her in Appleton. Not even the desire to watch the next night's game.

Climbing into her bed after only removing her shoes, she closed her eyes and drifted to sleep.

The shrill buzzing of her cell phone jolted her out of her dream a few hours later. She fumbled around trying to find it, but only managed to knock it from the nightstand table to the floor.

The buzzing finally stopped.

Kallie rolled and leaned over the side of the bed, reaching for her phone. After unplugging it from the charger, she got up and changed her clothes before going downstairs to the kitchen.

"Kallie." Dad finished pouring a mug of coffee and placed the carafe back on the warmer. "We weren't expecting you back until tomorrow."

"I know, Dad." She went to the fridge and grabbed the orange juice, then retrieved a glass from the cupboard. "Rafe was called up to the next level last night right after the game, so I just decided to come home instead."

She drained the glass, soothing the sore throat all the crying had given her, and filled it again.

"That's great news, right? He's one step closer to the majors?"

Nodding, she took another slow drink from the glass. "Yeah. He moved up from High-A to Double-A, whatever that means." She still had no understanding of the minor league.

"Next step is Triple-A, which I think is in Nashville. But he could get called up at any time."

"Daddy?" Kallie sat at the table and stared into her half-full glass. Something Rafe said yesterday really bothered her. Because he'd grown up with almost nothing, he'd adjusted to what he'd called the grueling conditions better than many of his teammates. "What do you think Rafe's chances are of making it that far?"

"I don't know, pumpkin." Dad sat next to her and sipped his coffee. "But I know that, if Rafe keeps working as hard as he is, he'll get the recognition he deserves."

"Daddy, I want to help him." She told him about the living conditions Rafe had to endure while she'd been with him in Appleton the last two days. "He shouldn't have to worry about paying for rent or food while he chases his dream. Our dream."

Dad studied her while he sipped his coffee. "What did you have in mind?"

"Well, since I'm living here and you and Mom aren't charging me rent, I wanted to send him part of my paychecks each month. And then, during the off-season, he could live here and train at a local fitness center."

"I don't know, Kallie. Are you sure that's wise?"

"What if I consider it an investment in our future?"

"We'll have to see."

Kallie knew that Rafe wouldn't just accept the handouts. Call it Stubborn Man Syndrome, or whatever. Pride. Ego. But she was determined to help him out in every way she could.

"Are you hungry?" Dad asked. "Would you like some pancakes?"

Kallie grinned. "I'll never turn down your pancakes, Daddy."

Mom walked into the kitchen while Dad was prepping the batter. "Kallie! I thought you were staying until tomorrow."

"Change of plans, obviously." Kallie saluted Mom with her glass.

"Rafe was called to the Double-A team in Mississippi last night, so she came home after the game."

Mom frowned. "You drove all that way in the dark?"

"I'm fine, Mom. It really wasn't that bad." Compared to how Rafe was living practically in squalor with the rest of his teammates, she was royalty. "I didn't want to stay without him."

The first plops of wet batter sizzled when they connected with the hot surface of the skillet as Kallie and Mom talked. She explained how she wanted to help Rafe with his finances. Mom expressed the same reservations Dad had not twenty minutes ago.

Grabbing her phone, Kallie looked up the Double-A location in Mississippi, then started searching the area on Google Maps.

While she ate breakfast, a kernel of an idea formed in her mind. While most of the minor league players were struggling just to make ends meet even during the season, there was no way she would let Rafe suffer any more than he already was.

She was determined to help him achieve his goals, no matter what the cost.

Chapter 18

Kallie entered the elegant restaurant ahead of Rafe, worried about how he'd be able to pay for their dinner.

Rafe had been called up to the Triple-A team in August, just two years after he'd been drafted and three months after he'd been bumped up to Double-A. Before he relocated to Tennessee, he stopped in La Crosse to treat Kallie to a celebratory dinner at The Waterfront, one of La Crosse's classiest restaurants.

"Thank you again for those amazing gifts." He helped her into her seat across from him. "My teammates were jealous that I have someone like you in my life."

"You're welcome." Kallie sipped her water. "I didn't think it was fair that you had to pay for a gym membership when you couldn't really afford it."

She remembered his less-than-ideal living conditions when she'd been in Appleton, and the gift cards she'd scrounged up to help him with training and his meal plan.

"I'm almost there." The triumph in his voice was unmistakable.

"You'll get there." She covered his hand with hers on the table. "You're the best on the team."

His grin turned lascivious. "Checkin' up on me, darlin'?"

"Always." Heat seared her cheeks. "I mean, I'm always seeing how you're doing. I want you to succeed, Rafe."

"I'm goin' to." He squeezed her hand.

"I have faith that you will."

He sipped his water. "How are your dreams coming along? Have you heard from any of the research hospitals?"

The waitress stopped by and took their order, then left as quickly as she arrived.

"Not yet. But it's only been a month. I'm sure I'll be hearing something within the next couple of weeks." With his encouragement, Kallie had applied again to the cancer research centers in Baltimore, Memphis and Madison. She figured she had a better shot now that she had eighteen months of experience under her belt.

"You can't give up on your dreams just to help me achieve mine." He'd said the same words to her when they'd spent the night on his air mattress in Appleton.

"I haven't," she countered, more vehemently than she intended. "I've just been …" she trailed off.

"You've been so focused on helping me with mine that yours have taken a backseat."

Kallie blushed. He'd hit the nail on the head. "Not entirely, no."

"Kallie," he scolded.

"What?" She looked up at him. He never called her by her given name anymore. "I'm not! I've applied to the hospitals again. I just haven't heard back."

"Have you followed up with them at all?"

Not really. "A couple of times. I just haven't heard from them."

"By the way, thank you for that keychain."

"I was wondering if you'd found it. You haven't said anything about it." The ball and glove she'd found at one of the stores in Appleton had been perfect. She'd stopped at one of the trinket stores that did custom engraving and had her initials plus the date inscribed on the back.

"Yeah. I found it in the pocket of my bat bag." He met her gaze with a playful smile. "I wonder how it got in there."

She raised an eyebrow. "I have no idea."

"Clever girl."

"I try to be." She sipped her drink. "How are things going off the field?"

"Thanks to you, I'm doing better than some of my teammates. That gym membership was probably the best thing anyone has done for me so far."

"What about a place to live?"

He shrugged. "I stayed with three other guys at a host family's house. Three grown men and only one bathroom. Not exactly ideal, but at least my performance on the field is getting recognized."

"You're amazing, Rafe."

"How are Noah and Justin doing?" She remembered meeting them in Appleton. Or, in Justin's case, seeing him again.

"They're following me to Nashville. We're gonna find a house to rent together there."

"Do you need another year's membership for that gym?" she asked.

"No. The one I have will carry over to a new city."

"What about food?" She didn't mention their current dinner or suggest going Dutch. She'd offer to pay for the whole bill, but she had a feeling he'd take offense.

"Good, thanks to that monthly subscription service you signed me up for."

She reached for his hand again. "I just want to take care of my guy."

He squeezed her fingers. "You're doing that and then some."

"I'm glad. I just worry about you, y'know?"

"I know." He looked up and met her gaze. "Is this all worth it? Do you have any regrets waiting for me?"

Kallie didn't hesitate. "I can't believe you'd ask me that. Of course it's all worth it. Because I have faith that all of our sacrifices now will pay off in the end."

The waitress dropped off their dinner shortly afterwards, and Rafe steered the conversation into less volatile channels by entertaining her with antics from some of his teammates.

Kallie told him about the night they were out shooting pool and met Amy's new boyfriend.

As Kallie figured, Rafe insisted on taking care of the bill when it arrived.

"Thanks to you, Kals, I have been able to save up a bit of a nest egg with what little I earned this summer," he chastised. "I wouldn't have brought you here if I couldn't have afforded it otherwise. You've given me so much already. At least let me give you this."

So she didn't argue.

That evening had ended with a very unsatisfying make-out session that left her wanting more. Of everything.

Riding high after a hard-fought win against the division leaders, Rafe and the other players laughed and joked as they returned to the locker room to shower and change.

"Larson!" Coach's booming voice echoed off the walls. "My office. Now!"

"Well, boys," Howie Larson sneered. "Looks like I'm up for a promotion. Later, losers."

He sauntered to the office where Coach and the team's GM were waiting. Their stoic expressions gave nothing away. The GM shut the blinds as Howie entered the room and closed the door.

"That doesn't sound good," Justin mumbled.

One of the pitchers, Ortiz, draped an arm over Justin's shoulder. "I don't think he's getting promoted."

"I wonder what he did this time." Noah scratched his chin.

Ortiz guffawed. "What hasn't he done! Maybe they're finally sick of his crap."

Of the players that had made it to Triple-A with Rafe, Howie had been the highest drafted and had the largest signing bonus. In his opinion, the outfielder had more to lose, and should have conducted himself accordingly.

"Who knows?" Rafe finished packing his gear. "I just wish he'd leave me alone."

Justin sat on the bench next to Rafe. "Honestly, with his attitude, I'm surprised he made it this far."

Rafe and his teammates murmured agreement, even as a subdued hush descended in the locker room.

Any time a player got called into what had been dubbed 'the principal's office' was somber – either a guy's dreams were coming true or getting crushed.

Based on Howie's attitude and lackluster playing this past season, Rafe had a feeling the outfielder's days with Tennessee were over. He grabbed his gear. "I'll see you guys at home."

"Aren't you gonna wait?" Noah pointed to the office.

Rafe shook his head. "I'm sure you hens will fill me in later."

His teammates' chuckles followed him to the exit.

In the parking lot Rafe walked to his car and dug out his cell phone, bringing up the speed dial for Kallie. It had been a month since they last talked – other than through voice mail – and he missed her dearly.

He climbed behind the wheel of his ancient Outback – a holdover from high school – and stuck the key into the ignition, but didn't crank the motor. Instead, he contemplated calling his girlfriend.

Even with the time difference it was still late, and he didn't want to wake her if she was sleeping.

His phone buzzed in his hand before he could hit Send. The number flashing on the screen made his heart drop to his stomach.

Return to the clubhouse. Now.

Snagging the keys from the ignition, Rafe stepped out of the car. He pocketed his wallet, keys and phone, then went back inside with heavy tread. Once inside the clubhouse, he retraced his steps to the locker room, right toward his antagonistic teammate.

"Hey, Donny Boy," Larson jeered, his face contorted into an angry mask. "Good luck. I heard you're next."

Shrugging off the outfielder's words, Rafe entered the locker room. The mood among the lingering players was even more subdued than when he'd left. He glanced at Larson's cubby on his way to Coach's office, which was completely empty.

He'd been cut!

Mixed emotions swam through Rafe's head as he crossed the room. Shock and disbelief because, for all his faults, Howie Larson was still a good player. Relief, sure, because now Rafe wouldn't have to endure Larson's bullying.

Dread overrode them all, as a stark reminder that nothing at any level of the minors was guaranteed.

He gripped the knob with clammy fingers and turned. The door eased open silently and he slipped inside, his guts clenching in fear.

Chapter 19

'Big changes are comin', Kals. Keep being patient.'

Kallie recalled Rafe's last words to her before he'd hung up from their last conversation two weeks ago. He'd sounded distracted during the call, and they hadn't talked for more than a few minutes – the shortest time they'd talked in the sixteen months since he was promoted to Triple-A in Tennessee.

They still exchanged daily texts. It seemed like every day she found something she wanted to share with him, and vice versa.

But she couldn't help wondering if she'd somehow upset him. Even with his texts, he seemed rather distant with her.

Maybe he really was distracted by the 'big changes' he'd alluded to. Or maybe he was upset with her because she'd been unable to attend any of his games in Nashville. And when she'd asked him to spend Christmas with her family, he'd brushed her off.

Kallie's phone buzzed with an incoming text.

We're having a girls' night. Dress warm but nice. See you at six!

The mattress rippled when Kallie plopped down onto her waterbed, a gift from her aunt and uncle after they'd purchased a new air bed.

She read the message again, pondering Amy's cryptic words. She typed out her reply.

I don't feel like going out. Have fun with Harley instead.

Kallie's stomach twisted in knots as she sent her next message to Rafe.

I'm sorry if I upset you when I asked you to spend Christmas with my family. I just wanted to see you again. Happy holidays. Good luck next season.

Moments after she hit send, her phone rang.

"I'm sorry, Amy —" she started.

"You are not canceling." Amy cut her off. "I've been planning this night for two weeks. I won't let you blow me off."

"We can go out another night," Kallie said. "No big deal."

"Nope. You're coming with me, whether you like it or not. I'll be there at six. Be ready."

"Why is this so important to you?" Kallie snapped, using anger to mask her pain.

"Because it is," Amy countered. "Be ready."

Amy disconnected the call.

Tears filled Kallie's eyes. *Oh, great. Now I've upset my boyfriend and my best friend.*

A text came in. Kallie saw that it was from Rafe.

You didn't upset me, Kals. I just made other arrangements, is all. I'm sorry I didn't tell you first.

It's okay, she typed back. *I'll see you when I see you. Night.*

Maintaining a long-distance relationship for three years had drained most of Kallie's energy, patience, and faith. Hearing his voice over the phone wasn't as satisfying as it used to be.

He'd said "I love you" at the end of their last call, but she started wondering if it was by rote instead of heartfelt.

He just said big changes were coming. Did his Christmas plans involve someone other than Florinda? Had Kallie missed the signs that he'd been drifting away? Were they headed for Splitsville?

Her heart cracked and a tear slipped down her cheek. Had he somehow stopped loving her while he'd been slogging it out in the minors? Maybe one of those ball bunnies had finally turned his head.

Suddenly Kallie felt less like going out and more like snuggling beneath the blankets and wallowing in an uncharacteristic bout of self-pity. It didn't help that again her application had been rejected by all three of the research hospitals she'd been trying to get into since graduating from college.

The doorbell rang promptly at six. Kallie jumped, though she'd been expecting it.

Again, she sent a text to Amy begging off for the night. Moments later footsteps stomped up the stairs and Kallie's bedroom door burst open.

"Why aren't you dressed?" Amy closed the door and leaned against it. "I told you to be ready by six."

"And I told you I wasn't going." Kallie couldn't understand her friend's anger. "I said we'd go out another night."

She tried shrugging it off, but Amy was having none of it.

"You are coming out with me, and that's that." Amy crossed her arms and leaned against the door. "Put on that burgundy sweater dress. It looks killer on you."

"You still haven't told me why, or where we're going."

"Do I need a reason to plan a night out with my best friend?" Amy fired back.

Kallie's knees went weak as the fight drained out of her and she sank back onto the bed. "I guess not."

"Good. You have ten minutes." Amy opened the door again. "If you're not downstairs, I'm coming back up."

Kallie walked to the window and glanced outside. Winter had come early to Wisconsin. The temps hovered in the low twenties, and there was just enough of a breeze to add a nip to the air. Four inches of snow already blanketed the ground, courtesy of a storm that blew through last weekend.

A bright, near-full moon had cleared the horizon and cast long shadows among the trees, the snow glistening softly beneath the moonbeams. Across the street, the neighbor's house was all decked out and ready for Christmas in its multi-hued glow. Everything looked so…normal.

Yeah, she'd rather curl up with a mug of hot cocoa and a good book. Or Rafe.

Another shaft of pain pierced her heart.

If I am about to lose Rafe…

Kallie couldn't finish the thought. Maybe going out with Amy was just the distraction she needed. Her mood lightened a little, though her heartache remained.

She grabbed the burgundy sweater dress from the dresser and quickly changed, cinching a wide, black, patent-leather belt around her waist. In deference to the cold, she pulled on some athletic leggings before stuffing her feet into knee-high winter boots.

With just four minutes left, she opted to leave her long, auburn hair down and covered her ears with a knitted headband.

After swiping on some mocha lipstick and brown-black mascara, she grabbed her purse and flew down the stairs with thirty seconds to spare.

Amy was waiting for her in the living room. She reached into her purse, extracted an expensive-looking vellum envelope and handed it to Kallie.

"What's this?" Kallie asked, taking the envelope and turning it over in her fingers. Only her name was written on it.

"Open it," Amy said.

Rolling her eyes, Kallie broke the wax seal and removed a matching card, then scanned the riddle printed on one side.

"What does it say?" Amy asked.

"Didn't you write it?" Kallie thrust the card into her friend's hands. "I'm not in the mood for riddles."

"Who killed your festive spirit?" Olivia bounded into the living room and stole the card from Amy. "It's a scavenger hunt!" she exclaimed. "Kallie, you love scavenger hunts."

"Honey, what's the matter?" Mom asked, coming in from the kitchen. "You were fine up until a couple of hours ago. What's changed?"

Everything. But she wasn't ready to talk about it, which didn't leave her many options. She snatched the card from Olivia and marched to the front door. "Fine. Let's go solve the stupid riddle."

"Kallie Marie, what has gotten into you?" her mother scolded, but Kallie was already shutting the door behind her.

"Don't worry," Amy said while Kallie was still within earshot. "I'll take care of her."

An icy blast hit Kallie in the face a second before Amy joined her outside.

"Are you cooled down?" she asked.

"Amy, what's going on?" Kallie demanded.

"Are you really interested in finding out?" she asked.

Kallie eyed her friend, then sighed in defeat. "Honestly I don't know what I want anymore."

"What's wrong?" Amy's tone changed.

"I'm missing Rafe," she said, seeing sympathy in her friend's eyes. "It's been two weeks since we last talked, and I think he might have found someone else."

"Why do you say that?" Amy grimaced as another gust nearly knocked them over. "Can we at least sit in the car and talk?"

"Or we can go inside, make hot chocolate and talk in my room," Kallie said hopefully.

"Sorry, girl." Amy laughed. "You have a riddle to solve."

Kallie hesitated. "I'm not feeling up to it."

"Maybe it'll help you take your mind off of Rafe." Amy tugged her toward the car.

"Ames, He's all I *can* think about." Tears stung Kallie's eyes again.

"Well, sitting around and moping won't make him come back," Amy stated. "Hell, it won't even make you feel better." She unlocked the doors and they climbed into the sporty coupe. "Now, what did the card say?"

Kallie read the riddle again. "'Red and green, wreaths of fire. Come find me, your heart's desire.' What does it mean?"

"What's red and green?" Amy asked.

"Freddy Krueger's sweater?" Kallie snickered. "Maybe the answer is on Elm Street."

"Maybe." Amy laughed. "If Freddy's your heart's desire. What else is red and green?"

Kallie pondered the clue again, her eyes darting around to the decorated houses. "Green wreaths have red bows on them."

"And where's the biggest wreath in the city?" Amy prompted.

"City Hall."

Amy shifted into gear and drove toward Main Street. Two minutes later she parked in front of Onalaska City Hall, which also housed the police and fire stations.

Kallie's boots crunched across the snow as she cut a path to the wreath. She scanned the ground, nearly missing the envelope attached to the back of the stand. She pulled the tie on the string and took the envelope back to the car. After buckling the seatbelt, she tore open the paper and extracted the card.

"'Kicking and Screaming, by East or by west. You'll find me here, because I'm the best.'" Kallie read the clue out loud. "East is capitalized."

"What? Like a name or something?"

"Hmm." Kallie wondered. "East Avenue?"

"Kicking and Screaming. Wasn't that a Will Ferrell movie?"

"Soccer!" Kallie laughed. "OmniCenter. The soccer fields."

Amy pulled away from the curb and turned right on Fourth Avenue. "Does this mean you're feeling better?"

"A little, I guess." Kallie's smile faded a bit. "I'm scared, Ames. What if following our dreams has torn us apart?"

What if waiting for him the past three years has been all for nothing?

"But what if it hasn't been? What if you're exactly where you need to be at the exact moment you need to be there?" Amy drummed her fingers on the steering wheel. "There's a box of tissues behind the seat."

Pondering her friend's words, Kallie reached back and grabbed a couple of sheets, dabbing her eyes to keep her makeup intact. The pretense of trying to be ladylike was destroyed when a loud goose-honk blasted the air as she blew her nose. Amy laughed as she turned into the parking lot between the snow-covered fields.

A piece of paper fluttered in the breeze, threatening to break free from its binding. Kallie saw it right away and pointed. "There."

Amy braked to a stop in front of the shelter gate and Kallie jumped out, a sharp blast of icy air freezing the tears that had dampened her cheeks.

Ripping the envelope from the string, she dashed back to the car. Wasting no time, she tore open the flap and pulled out the card. "'Across the bridge and over the tracks, our love is like a river. Pedaling forward, never holding back.'" She thought for a moment, her enthusiasm growing with each riddle. Her mind whirled. "Bike trail."

Amy laughed. "Which one?"

"Let's see." Kallie scanned the riddle again. "River. Bridge. Highway Sixteen."

Amy turned left onto Riders Club Road and headed for Sand Lake Road, then took the on-ramp for the freeway. "Why do you think Rafe is pulling away?"

Kallie shrugged, her depression threatening to close in again. "Just something he said the last time we talked."

"What was it?" she asked softly.

The concern in Amy's voice brought the tears back to her eyes. "We talked for all of two minutes. He said big changes were coming, and then he had to go." Kallie wiped her nose with the tissue. "We haven't talked since."

"Oh, hon. Hang in there, okay?" Amy made the right-turn onto the highway and darted into the far-left lane.

"There's the bridge." Kallie pointed as they neared the stop lights.

Amy steered into the left lane and turned with the arrow. She parked in the space closest to the entrance of the trail and dug a small but powerful flashlight from the glove box.

Kallie exited the car and swept the bright beam over the ground. She saw several fresh footprints in the snow, but only one set veered toward the bridge over the railroad tracks.

Despite the brightness of the LEDs, she couldn't be sure if the tracks were male or female. The size could have gone either way, the tread pattern indistinct.

Following the footsteps, she spotted the envelope tied to the rail. The wind cut through her leggings as she snatched it and ran back to the car, her teeth chattering. Her fingers shook from the cold, and she almost couldn't open the flap.

"You okay?" Amy asked.

"F-f-f-fine. Just c-c-cold."

Amy turned the heater up full-blast. Kallie rubbed her hands together, blowing hot air into the small opening between her thumbs to return some warmth to her hands.

"What does it say?" Amy asked.

Kallie's fingers still trembled, but she finally managed to break the seal. "I hope you have enough gas," she replied. "This is turning into one hell of a scavenger hunt."

Chapter 20

"'The mountain of love is a slippery slope. Don your skis and don't lose hope.'" The card fluttered in Kallie's numb fingers as she read it. "I think we're going to Mt. La Crosse."

Amy laughed. "I think so too."

Hot air from the vents seeped through her snow-covered leggings as Kallie relaxed and leaned her head against the seat. As Amy turned left onto the highway and headed south, Kallie closed her eyes and huddled deeper into her coat.

"You weren't kidding," Amy said some time later. "This is quite the trek."

Kallie opened her eyes. The glare of the lights in the Big Lots! parking lot made her wince. "Why are we doing this?" she asked, her curiosity getting the better of her. The way Amy insisted on dragging her along, she wondered if maybe her friend had set up the clues. But she seemed as excited about the riddles as Kallie. Amy couldn't be that good of an actress.

Could she?

Or was it someone else that had set it up? Her heart hoped it was Rafe.

"Because it's fun?" Amy shrugged. "It beats staying inside, right?"

"We'd be a lot warmer inside," Kallie muttered. "Obviously someone went through a lot of trouble. So far, the clues have been out in the open. Anyone could have walked off with them."

"Well, I think we should see where they lead." Amy bit her lip. "You're right. Someone did put a lot of thought into this for us. Let's enjoy it."

"But who?" None of the cards were signed, and all were typed on basic cardstock. Nothing extraordinary about any of them so far. Anxiety swamped her as Amy turned into the parking lot of the pro shop and lounge. Kallie climbed out and looked around. "Now what?"

"I dunno." Amy shrugged. "Maybe we should go inside and ask."

Kallie snorted. "Yeah right. 'Excuse me, please. Have you seen an envelope addressed to someone named Kallie Huntington?'"

"As a matter of fact," came a voice from behind them. Kallie jumped.

"Sorry, miss," the man said as she spun around. "Didn't mean to scare you."

Kallie studied him. He looked a lot like Justin, Rafe's teammate from when they'd played for the Loggers. "It's fine." She shrugged it off.

"I was saying that there's something for Kallie in the bar next to the pro shop." His teeth gleamed white beneath the bright lights of the slopes.

"Thanks." Amy grabbed Kallie's arm.

"That was weird," Kallie said as they entered the building and made their way to the lounge. "He looked just like Justin."

"Who?"

"Never mind," she said as they crossed the lounge to the bar.

"What can I get for you ladies?" The man was tall and dark-haired. Like Rafe.

Pain pierced her heart, but Kallie tamped it down. "I believe you have something for Kallie Huntington."

"That's you?" At her nod, he said, "I believe this also comes with two mugs of hot cocoa." He handed her a small gift-wrapped box and went to fix their drinks.

Kallie tore open the silver paper and flipped up the hinged lid. 'To match your eyes. Please wear this.' was inscribed on the small card. When she lifted it, she saw the most stunning necklace. "Oh, wow."

Wrought in either silver or white gold, diamonds and amethysts glistened, the stones set in a floral pattern around the chain. Rafe's image popped into her head. *If he's about to break up with me, why would he buy it?* Did she perhaps have another secret admirer? Or maybe it was from Rafe and she'd completely misinterpreted their last phone conversation.

"Oh, that's gorgeous!" Amy exclaimed. "Here. Let me help."

Ignoring Kallie's protests, Amy grabbed the box and extracted the necklace, then clasped the chain around Kallie's neck.

"That's beautiful," the bartender said, passing them each an insulated mug filled with cocoa, twin trails of steam rising from the lids. "Your friend has excellent taste."

"I agree," Amy said. "Hey, there's another envelope with the necklace."

How did she know? Kallie's fingers shook as she lifted the foam and extracted the card. She ripped open the flap, and sighed as she scanned the clue. The next destination seemed like a let-down compared to the necklace and hot chocolate.

"What's it say?" the bartender asked.

"'We are six with foamy heads. A world record that still stands.'" She met Amy's gaze.

"The World's Largest Six-Pack." Amy chuckled. "I guess it's time to go."

"I guess so." When they got back to the car, she asked, "How many of these are left?"

"How should I know?" Amy glanced at Kallie as she turned onto the highway and headed for the City Brewery. "Why? Aren't you having fun?"

Kallie fingered the necklace, some of the joy in the riddles leeching from her. "It's such an extravagant gift. I almost don't want to keep it." She racked her brain, trying to think of anyone else who would set up the scavenger hunt for her, in case Rafe wasn't actually behind the riddles. Had Amy's boyfriend set them up for her instead? She dismissed the idea. Amy's eyes were brown, not violet-blue like her own. Rafe seemed the only logical choice. Hope blossomed in her chest and erased some of her doubt.

"Kallie, the person who chose it picked it for you," Amy scolded. "The card said it would match your eyes, and they were right."

"The last time I talked to Rafe, he was still playing Tennessee. Minor league players don't make a lot of money." She'd seen first-hand how Rafe had struggled to make ends meet, even with the gifts she'd sent him.

Amy cocked her brow, her vision never leaving the road. "How do you know that?"

"Rafe told me." Kallie shrugged. "That's why we waited, so he could get the hard part over with first and get up to the big leagues."

"Maybe he succeeded."

Again, Kallie shrugged. "What if he didn't?"

"But what if he did?"

Rafe hadn't been very forthcoming with details about his contract negotiations during the off-season, and she hadn't asked. Her last check of the website still had him on the active roster in Tennessee.

Recognizing the futility in arguing with Amy, Kallie crossed her arms and let the subject drop. Fifteen minutes later Amy turned into the parking lot of the City Brewery Hospitality Center and Kallie grabbed the flashlight. She sprinted to the 54-feet-tall silos decorated like giant cans of beer, the stench of burnt hops from the nearby krausening cellars heavy in the night air.

Wrinkling her nose, she scanned the sign declaring the holding tanks the world's largest six-pack as a statue of King Gambrinus saluted her with his golden goblet from across the street. But she saw no trace of the envelope on or around the sign denoting the landmark. A flutter from the steps caught her attention as she rounded the corner of the building. She trudged over, snow glistening beneath the bright beam. In the slight breeze, the envelope tugged at its moorings on the metal handrail attached to steps leading to the side entrance.

Again, Kallie noticed the footprints, similar in size and tread to those on the bridge. She compared the impression to her own. The sizes were almost identical. *A woman? It has to be.* "That's way too small for a man," she muttered. Again, she wondered if Amy had planted the clues. She'd said she'd spent two weeks planning for tonight. Was she in on this with Rafe? What waited for her at the end of the final clue?

"Excuse me, miss?" someone asked behind her.

For the second time in twenty minutes Kallie jumped. He gave her an apologetic smile. "I was ..." she faltered.

"Breaking and entering?" He wore some kind of uniform, though it sounded like he was teasing her.

She laughed, because the concept was ludicrous. "No. Picking this up." She held the envelope. "Do you by chance work here?"

"Yes, I do." He tipped his cap. "Fifteen years now."

She tapped the card with her finger. "Did you happen to see who might've left this?"

The man took it, studying it before handing it back. "No, sorry."

"Thanks anyway." Kallie accepted the envelope back and headed to the car.

"What took you so long?" Amy asked.

"I – I had trouble finding it." She ripped the seam, her fingers shaking from the cold as she read the card. "We're going to the Southside Oktoberfest grounds."

"How do you know?" Amy furrowed her brow. "What does the card say?"

"'Wilkommen to our Haus, where Gemütlechkeit reigns supreme,'" she read, deliberately butchering the German words. Amy giggled as she finished reading. "'Carnival and Ein Prosit, maple leaves and thee.'"

Amy started the car, still laughing. "How do you know it's the Southside grounds?"

"Makes the most sense," she reasoned. "More secure places to hide the card."

"Southside it is." Amy backed out of the parking spot and turned left onto Fourth Street.

"Ames, I don't know how many more of these I can do." She blinked back tears. "I'm freezing my buns off for what? What's the prize at the end of all of this?" At least with the medallion hunts they knew what the end reward would be. This time she had no idea what was at the end. *Maybe that's why I'm losing excitement. What will I do if Rafe isn't waiting for me?*

"Let's do one more, okay?" Amy cranked the heater again. "Maybe it'll be the last one."

"I hope so." Kallie sipped her cocoa, the heat from the mug warming her frozen hands.

"You never know," Amy said. "It might be a brand new car!"

Kallie giggled at the cheesy game show line.

Again, Rafe's image appeared in front of her. He was smiling, like the last time she'd been in his arms when he'd played in Appleton. His body had been more solid thanks to his stringent workout routine, and definitely more defined. She desperately wanted him to be the one behind the notes. *What if he is waiting for me?* Would he propose? Or what if he made it to the majors and this was his way of sharing the excitement with her?

Amy turned the car into the parking area in front of the main entrance and Kallie went in search of the clue. She found it tucked into the slats of the window shutter closest to the main entrance. Fighting a gust of icy air, she dashed back to the car and tore it open.

A tear slid down her cheek and landed on the card, blurring the ink and her vision. "I'm done." Fumbling with the clasp of the necklace, she slipped it from her neck. "Take me home."

"What?" Amy sounded panicked. "No!"

"It's not the last clue." Kallie sniffed. "But I'm done playing. My butt is freezing, and I'm tired of trudging through snow to get these silly little cards."

"Wait." Amy rested a hand on Kallie's arm. "What did the card say?"

"It doesn't matter! Forget the ride. I'll walk." She groped for her purse through the blinding tears and pushed out of the car, hustling down the street toward the bus depot.

"Kallie!"

Kallie huddled deeper into her coat, pulling up the hood against the wind.

The businesses around her were decorated for the holidays, but she couldn't appreciate anything beyond the pain in her heart. Kallie never made it to a bus stop. She sat down on a bench in front of the Radisson Hotel and gave in to the sobs racking her body.

Kallie didn't know how much time had passed since her break-down. Her whole body was numb, the tears cathartic. Slowly she became aware of her surroundings.

"We need to tell her," a familiar voice said nearby. "She's a wreck." The voice paused. "Then you might want to wait." Another pause. "Give me thirty minutes."

Kallie looked around with gritty eyes, blinking in disbelief. "Ames?" she croaked past the lump in her throat.

"I'm sorry, Kallie." Amy hugged her. "I wanted to say something at the ski lodge, but–"

"You're in on this – this goose chase?" she asked.

Amy nodded. "I planted the clues and the necklace." She held out the box. "It's yours. I know who it's from, and they want you to have it."

"Who?"

"I'm under orders to not spoil the surprise." Amy's lips twisted. "But it's someone who cares about you very much."

Kallie sniffed, wiping her eyes with her coat sleeve, but otherwise said nothing.

"Are you interested in finding out?" Amy asked gently.

"I'd probably scare them away." Kallie gave a half-hearted laugh. "I must look like Bride of Frankenstein."

"You don't look like a raccoon, but your eyes and nose are puffy and red," Amy said. "We don't have time for a total makeover, but let's see if we can't fix some of the damage."

"Thanks a lot." But Kallie was too drained emotionally to put any heat behind it.

"Come on. Let's get you cleaned up." Amy guided her up Main Street. "Would you like more hot chocolate?"

The numbness wore off and Kallie began shaking. "S-s-soup, p-p-please."

Amy guided her to their favorite sushi bistro a block away and ordered a bowl of miso soup while Kallie took advantage of the facilities.

Nearly screeching upon seeing her reflection, Kallie dabbed some hand soap onto a paper towel and washed her face, then applied a cold compress to her puffy eyes. Digging in her handbag, she unearthed a comb and raked it through her windswept curls. She couldn't fix all of her makeup, but she reapplied mascara and her mocha lipstick.

Amy popped her head in the door. "You're looking better. Your soup's ready."

"I'll be right out."

"Hurry up. We're on a time crunch."

Kallie remembered Amy saying thirty minutes on the phone earlier. She swiped the comb one more time through her hair and joined her friend at the bar in the restaurant. Amy sat on a stool, her back to the restrooms and her phone up to her ear.

Amy hung up her cell phone as Kallie sat on the stool next to her. "Feel better?"

"A little." Kallie sipped the soup, the bowl warming her hands.

"Well enough to continue?" Amy asked.

A flash of irritation bolted through Kallie as she took another drink of soup. "Let me guess. I have to solve the riddle." She couldn't keep the frustration from her tone.

Various diners sat at the tables scattered about, some talking and laughing, other couples holding hands and smiling. One couple playfully attempted to attack each other with their chopsticks.

Amy touched her arm. "Someone went through a lot of trouble to set this up." She retrieved the necklace from her purse and slid it across the counter. "That person really cares about you, and they're doing this as a way of showing how much."

"Why the riddles?" Kallie asked. "Why not say 'meet me here at eight'?"

"The person who arranged this *knows* you, Kallie," Amy implored. "They know you enjoy scavenger hunts and solving puzzles. How many times have we hunted for the Oktoberfest medallion?"

Kallie slumped as defeat swamped her.

Amy rubbed her back. "What's wrong?"

"I guess I'm still worried about Rafe," she confessed. She wanted to believe that Rafe was waiting for her at the end, but their last conversation had been brief and tense. She didn't know if she fit into his future anymore.

"Do you think he's broken up with you?"

Kallie hugged her abdomen as daggers of pain pierced her heart.

"Answers that question," Amy said dryly. "Well, I think there's only one way to find out." She grabbed Kallie's purse.

"Hey!" Kallie slapped her friend's hand. "What are you doing?"

Amy had the audacity to laugh at her. "It's about time you busted out of your funk. Finish your soup, and let's solve the last riddle."

Grumbling, Kallie polished off the bowl of lukewarm miso, scooping the tofu and seaweed bits with chopsticks. "Okay, what's the last clue?" she asked, setting the empty bowl on the counter as Amy retrieved the envelope.

Kallie took the clue from her friend and read it out loud. "'For love, it is the season. One last stop…here's four million reasons.'" Having something to work out helped to somewhat take her mind off Rafe. "The season," she pondered. "Four million reasons. What about a bank? The four million could refer to money. Maybe Rafe got a four-million-dollar bonus, which means he made it to the majors."

"Could be," Amy said thoughtfully. "But I don't think that's it."

She didn't immediately dismiss the idea, since they were across the street from a bank high-rise. She mumbled beneath her breath, trying to work out what else could involve four million individual parts. "I don't think cars would have that many pieces."

"They could," Amy agreed, "but they're not directly associated with any seasons."

"Is the clue related to Christmas?"

"Well, to winter and the holidays," Amy conceded.

"Okay. So, we have four million parts or pieces related to winter, and a season for love," Kallie summarized, looking out onto Main Street. Lights blinked on the tree in the lobby of the bank across from the restaurant. "Duh. Rotary Lights."

"Let's go." Amy paid the tab and they stepped out into the frigid evening. "It might be easier to walk to Riverside Park. It's only a few blocks."

"Why? Where are you parked?"

"In the ramp." She pointed to the building next to the bank. "Second floor."

Kallie huddled deeper into her heavy coat. "Might as well. I can't get much colder."

Snowflakes danced on the swirling currents as the cold winter wind bit at her exposed skin. Since 1995, the local Rotary clubs turned Riverside Park into a magical Christmas wonderland. Thousands of strands of lights weaved between the trees, and animated displays stood at random intervals around the lane. They'd started out with just two hundred and fifty thousand lights. Now that number topped four million.

Kallie usually loved Christmas, and seeing the park all decked out with millions of twinkling lights was her favorite attraction. But anxiety overrode her emotions. She tried to enjoy the festive displays as they passed, but Amy had grabbed her and they started jogging through the park. The woman was on some kind of mission.

"Slow down!" Kallie tried tugging at her wrist.

Amy's grip tightened. "We can't!"

A mix of emotions flooded through Kallie as they dodged other people walking through the park. Anticipation of the end, but also a little dread that it was almost over. "Where's Rafe?"

"You'll see," Amy said again, propelling Kallie through the park toward the recently reconstructed bandshell. The open concrete structure, even with its wood and copper roof, provided little shelter against the elements, but Kallie ascended the wide, shallow risers of the stage anyway.

Whether Amy realized it or not, she'd just revealed that Rafe had a role in the scavenger hunt. Hope uncurled inside Kallie, but her doubts refused to let it grow.

"So, what am I supposed to do here?" she asked.

"Wait." Amy dashed off again.

"I'm going to kill her," Kallie muttered, her breath a puff of white vapor in the frigid air. A strong gust of wind whistled through the openings between the tree trunk columns holding the roof as it blew across the landscape from the river. She shoved her hands into her pockets as she leaned against the wall at the back of the stage.

She kicked the concrete in frustration with the heel of her boot as she looked around the park. Thousands of miles of lights dangled from every tree branch. A rope-light train chugged, and the arms of a windmill turned with an invisible motor. On the side nearest the river, an animated squirrel darted up and over the trees, an acorn clenched in its teeth.

A continuous stream of cars crawled past at a snail's pace as their occupants took in the displays. Others walked the ribbons of sidewalk winding through the landscape. Shouts and laughter echoed from the skating rink occupants halfway up the park. Christmas music blared from various speakers around the area.

At the north end of the park in front of the Convention and Visitor's Bureau, displays danced and lights flashed in time with music from a local radio station. A lighted display of the La Crosse Queen churned its red paddlewheel across the snow.

"I'm going to kill her," Kallie muttered again as she pushed away from the wall with her heel. "I'm gonna kill them both for putting me through this." She descended the risers toward stage front with the intention of finding Amy, when she heard the soft whinny of a horse and the nicker of the accompanying driver offering carriage rides. A familiar face at the bottom of the steps stopped her in her tracks. She gasped, tears stinging her eyes as she covered her mouth with her hand.

"Hello, Kallie."

"Rafe?" The word slipped out on a whisper. She blinked, afraid he was an apparition that would disappear into the swirling flakes. She slipped on a small patch of ice on the concrete.

Rafe caught her in his arms. "Easy, darlin'."

A lone tear froze on her cheek as she wound her arms around his neck, inhaling his familiar scent. "What are you doing here?"

"I had to see you. I missed you so much." Rafe kissed her lips. "That necklace looks so beautiful on you."

"I missed you, too." The last three years had been agony, only being able to hear his sexy drawl when their schedules had permitted. Especially once he'd started playing in Milwaukee's farm system. "I've been so scared."

He didn't loosen his grip around her waist. "Why?"

"The –" she sniffed. "The last time we talked. I was afraid you didn't want me anymore."

"I'm so sorry, darlin'. I never wanted to give you that impression." He released her and stepped back, cupping her cheeks with his palms. "I couldn't say much, because I'd been called up to the big dance."

Tears stung her eyes as the warmth of his hands seeped into her chilled flesh.

He cupped her cheeks in his gloved hands, brushing her tears with his thumbs. "Thank you for completin' the riddles."

She shrieked as happiness erased her frustration from the scavenger hunt. "The big – you mean you're going to play at American Family Field?"

Grinning, he nodded.

"Amy?" she asked.

"She told me about how much fun you had with those medallion hunts, and she was happy to help. These last years have been the best of my life," he continued. "Our time apart has shown me how much I want you by my side. You're my rock, the one constant that kept me going when my life was chaos." He kissed her again. "You're smart and gorgeous. I can't imagine not having you in my life." He dropped to one knee on the frozen pavement as he retrieved something from his coat pocket.

Omigod. The thought raced through her mind as lights glittered off the melted snow dusting his dark hair. A few people sat on the benches in front of the stage, curious to see what was happening.

Rafe flipped open the lid on the box in his hand. A purple amethyst glinted from the bed of satin, surrounded by a halo of diamonds. "Kallie Huntington, will you marry me?"

Tears spilled over, freezing on her cheeks. Kallie could only stare. She swallowed, but couldn't speak past the emotion clogging her throat. More people joined the crowd.

Rafe's lips twisted into a wry grin. "Help me out here, darlin'."

Kallie nodded as tears flowed faster.

"Come on, honey!" someone from the audience called. "Give the man an answer!"

Kallie laughed, sniffling at the same time. "Yes." She squealed. "Yes, yes, yes!"

Thunderous applause rose up from around them, but she barely registered the noise as their lips met in the best kiss they'd ever shared.

Suddenly the air didn't feel so cold.

THE END

About CJ Bower

Reading and writing have always been a huge part of CJ's life, and she's been creating stories since childhood. For as long as she can remember, she's been putting pen to paper and
creating complex characters in rich settings. With the support of wonderful family and friends, she finally decided to make the big leap into the world of professional publishing.

CJ lives in Western Wisconsin with her husband. They have one child of the four-legged and furry kind. When she's not working or writing, she enjoys baking, having picked up her first piping bag at fourteen. She started decorating full time at age twenty-three and spent four years in her family's bakery before returning to school. She also enjoys volunteering at the local animal rescue shelter and advocating for those who are unable to speak for themselves.

CJ's Website:
www.cjbowerauthor.wordpress.com

Reader email:
cjbowerauthor@hotmail.com

CityScapes: A sweet, romantic tour across the United States.

North Carolina:
Racing Away With His Heart:

Nisa Forester has avoided everything racing related since the violent crash that killed her father. Twenty years later, the track management has scheduled a memorial in his honor during the season's longest race, and she attends as a favor to her brother, Cole. Finding love is not at all on her radar.

Tyson Patterson sees Nisa for the first time at a pre-race party, annoyed that she attends with his biggest on-track rival. In an attempt to woo her away from Cole, Ty asks her to dance. However, as their relationship progresses after a case of mistaken identity, things get complicated between them.

Just as love blooms between them, Ty hits the wall next to the spot where her father did, giving Nisa a crash course on why she never wanted to fall for a racecar driver. Can she find the strength to overcome her fears? Will Ty be able to convince her that their love is worth the risk?

Wyoming:
Stuck in a Rut:

Susan Addington is at a crossroads in her life. She loves her job as the premier wedding photographer for NYC's elite, but lately she feels like she's been spinning her wheels. When her friend suggests a wagon train re-enactment tour in Wyoming, she jumps at the chance to get back to her roots as a nature photographer. She soon discovers that visiting still-visible landmarks along the Oregon Trail is like stepping back in time. And, oddly, coming home.

As her journey progresses from Fort Laramie to South Pass City, sparks flicker with the charming but mysterious Caleb McKnight, one of the tour group's employees. Through daily interaction, Susan becomes more attracted to Caleb, and she finds that he's not as immune to the chemistry between them as he appears.

Just as something more than friendship grows between them, they end up caught in the cross-hairs between danger and intrigue. Can Susan forgive Caleb for his role? And can this city girl and country boy find a compromise before they run out of trail? Or will they end up stuck in a rut forever?

Tennessee:

Music City Soiree:

Rocky Baker thought she was content with her modest, quiet life. Having grown up in the foster system, she kept mostly to herself. But a chance meeting with a lovely CNA gave her courage to open herself up to the residents of the Music City Senior Center. There, she met two amazing eighty-year-old women, whom she'd unofficially adopted as her grandmothers.

Alexander has no time, or desire, to focus on his personal life as he fights to rebuild his grandfather's legacy after his unscrupulous father nearly bankrupted it. When his grandmother introduces him to the new volunteer at the senior center, Alexander gives Rocky the cold shoulder, jealous of Rocky's place in his grandmother's heart.

After she's attacked one night while leaving her job, Alexander comes to Rocky's rescue. While she's in his care, they form a fragile friendship.

When the threads of trust are broken, can Rocky learn to heal and forgive? Will Alexander learn that family is more than blood bonds and make amends?

Caked With Pleasure Series

On Track with Icing (book 1):

She's everything he wanted in a woman...except for one thing.

Plus-sized bakery owner Jacqui Jacobson's confidence is at an all-time low after her public divorce and her ex-husband's despicable accusations. So the last person she expects to show interest in her is racing hot-shot Nick Barrister. But when the two click over her risqué cake designs, it seems like icing on the cake.

However, Jacqui hasn't told him that not being able to have children was the main cause for her marriage ending. As her relationship with Nick turns from casual to serious he expresses his desire for children, and now time is running out. Can she tell him first before her ex-husband, who has reared his ugly head and is determined to destroy her new-found happiness, beats her to it? And will Nick still want her once he finds out?

Content Warning: contains lots of steamy sexual content and exciting racing action.

Icing the Competition (book 2):

Can the innocent beauty heal the arrogant stock car driver's heart?

Shawn Sheldon comes home early from Daytona and discovers his wife Lisa in their bed with two men. He immediately kicks her out and files for divorce, but the hits keep blindsiding him like a high-speed crash at Talladega. Shattered by Lisa's betrayal, Shawn takes a self-imposed sabbatical to let his heart heal. However, a chance encounter with the beautiful Persephone encourages him to try again.

Persephone Williams has harbored a secret crush on Shawn since their introduction a year ago. While she's dated in the past, she's never had a steady boyfriend, and none of them inspired her to punch her V-card. After one hot, steamy kiss with Shawn, she finds herself giving in to the desires of her heart. He is arrogant—cocky even—but he proves that he has a soft side too.

When Shawn's ex-wife resurfaces and tries digging her red-lacquered talons into him again, he shows Peri that she's the one he wants. But can Peri handle his high-profile career and the media circus that goes with it?

Content Warning: contains steamy sex and hot racing action

Made in the USA
Monee, IL
11 May 2022